Praise for Julie Smith and her
REBECCA SCHWARTZ MYSTERIES

"An interesting new detective personality . . . Smith shows an Agatha Christie-like capacity for making much ado about clues, concocting straw hypotheses, and surprising us, in the end. . . . Smith's crisp storytelling, her easy knowledge of local practices, and her likable, unpredictable heroine will make readers look forward to more of sleuth Schwartz's adventures."
—*San Francisco Chronicle*

"A delightful modern sleuth."
—*Minneapolis Star & Tribune*

"Rebecca's lively first-person narration brands her a new detective to watch."
—*Wilson Library Bulletin*

"An attractive and amusing heroine."
—*The San Diego Union-Tribune*

OTHER PEOPLE'S SKELETONS

Julie Smith

IVY BOOKS • NEW YORK

Ivy Books
Published by Ballantine Books
Copyright © 1993 by Julie Smith

Library of Congress Catalog Card Number: 93-91589

ISBN 0-8041-1086-7

Printed in Canada

First Edition: November 1993

To Mittie, the best in the business

If not for the kindness and generosity of people like the following, books simply wouldn't get written. Many thanks to Steve Bryzman, Steve Holtz, Barry Gardner, Mary Jean Haley, Michael Patella, Jon Carroll, Brooke Smith, Officer Rose Melendez and Inspector Jim Bergstrom of the San Francisco Police Department and Sergeant John Hunt III of the Piedmont Police Department.

CHAPTER 1

I once said to one of my clients, a man who'd killed someone in self-defense, that it must have been the hardest thing he ever had to live through.

"Not even close," he said. "Not nearly as hard as my divorce. Learning that someone I thought I knew was so different; living with that. That's the hardest thing I ever had to do."

The night Chris Nicholson, my law partner, was nearly arrested for murder I started to see what he meant. It was a time when everything I thought about the world changed, everything I thought I knew about human beings and who they are turned upside down and inside out. And it was probably a change for the better.

I can say that now that it's over. I can even say that I think I'm a better person for it, a bigger and more aware person. I'm certainly a weirder person. But I notice I'm a little more careful about whom I call weird these days. Who among us is exactly like the rest of us? And more to the point, who hasn't got a secret? Even, maybe, a whole secret life.

I think I should go back to the old Rebecca for a moment here, just to illustrate the progression of the thing; the Rebecca of the Cosmic Blind Date.

I was standing in line at the post office one day, mailing a birthday present, a job it's not ethical to give to

my secretary—and anyway, he wouldn't do it. I was
impatient, in a hurry because I had to go home and
pack for a business trip to Seattle. And a man was staring at me. He was sort of a nice-looking man, in fact
a very nice-looking man, nothing wrong with him except that his hair was a little long and he was rumpled.
That could have meant nothing or a lot, like maybe he
was crazy and didn't care how he looked, or maybe he
was homeless and didn't have a mirror, which also
might have meant he was crazy. Without being narrow-
minded about it, most urban women would agree, I
think, that men who stare at you and might be crazy
are probably best avoided.

I was busily keeping my distance and avoiding eye
contact (or trying to) but I couldn't help it, I kept sneak-
ing little nervous glances to see if he was still staring.
And he was, every time.

Finally, he simply walked up to me and said, "Excuse me, I know this sounds crazy, but you aren't named
Rebecca, are you? By any chance?"

"Do we know each other?"

"You mean you *are*? I don't believe it—I'm scaring
myself."

"Apparently, you know me, but I don't know you."

"Well, I have to know one more thing. There's no
chance you're from Seattle, is there?"

Ordinarily, I'd have been too irritated to answer, but
it was so odd, his bringing up Seattle, that I blurted,
"No, but I'm going there tomorrow."

"Oh my God. Oh my *God*. I don't believe this."

"Excuse me," I said, as coldly as I could. By now I
was thoroughly sorry I hadn't called the nearest cop,
and it was my turn at the window.

He waited for me. When I turned back toward the
door, I saw that he had smoothed his hair and tucked

in his shirt. "I'm Max Bruner," he said, offering his hand and looking as normal as an oatmeal cookie. "I know you think I'm crazy, but I wonder if I could just talk to you for a minute. I teach religion at a college in Oregon." He stopped suddenly as if he'd had a brainstorm. "I know! Come and meet my wife."

"I beg your pardon?"

"She's right outside. Really. Waiting in the car."

Dazed, I walked out with him. "There she is." He pointed to a blue Nissan driven by a perfectly attractive, sensible-looking woman who looked as if she couldn't possibly be married to a crazy man. By this time I was a lot more curious than annoyed. I walked over with him.

"Dear, this is Rebecca . . ."

"Schwartz."

"Rebecca Schwartz. My wife, Lorraine. Honey, remember what those psychics told Roger DeCampo? About the dark-haired woman in the pink suit?"

"Ah, yes, the one named Rebecca."

"Well, I saw . . . uh . . . this lady in the post office and that was her name."

She looked dismayed. "But Roger's gone back to Seattle."

I was dark-haired, wearing a deep rose suit, and not at all liking the turn the conversation was taking.

"She's going there tomorrow."

Lorraine lit up. "I don't believe it; this is much too weird." It was obvious she thought it was a good kind of weird. "Tell her, Max."

He turned to me. "Well, we both just finished a six-week seminar over in Berkeley. Roger's a—well, a specialist in the Eastern religions. We hung out a lot this summer and Roger got it into his head to go to a psychic—being in Berkeley and all. And the psychic told him he'd meet a dark-haired woman in a pink suit with whom he'd have—get this—an 'important' relationship.''

I was starting to be amused. ''Oh, no. Not another learning experience.''

''The psychic said her name would be either Rosalind or Ruth, something like that. Well, he kind of got into it and went to another psychic and that one saw a woman in his life too, but all she said was that she was named Rebecca. So he asked what she looked like and sure enough, she was dark and wearing pink. So you know what he did?''

''Placed an ad in the *East Bay Express*.''

''No, he went to a third psychic. That one only said she'd be dark and about five-feet-five—how tall are you, Rebecca?''

''About that.''

Exactly that. I'd gone from amused to intrigued.

''But the only thing was, he looked all over Berkeley and couldn't find her. Then when I saw you, you so perfectly answered the description.''

Was this some kind of setup? Were these people trying to pull something? They could have been except for one thing—the business trip to Seattle had come up at the last moment. No one but my law partner and my travel agent even knew I was going.

Lorraine said, ''Why don't you give Rebecca Roger's phone number? What do you think, Rebecca? Would you want to call him?''

''Well, I don't know anything about him.''

They spent the next ten minutes singing the praises of their friend, who, aside from having a sterling character and all that, was lots of fun, ''especially for a professor,'' they said.

The upshot was, I said they could give him my number. I was listed, anyhow, and the whole thing was starting to look larkish. I was quite giddy with the encounter, shaking my head on the walk home and murmuring, "Only in San Francisco."

When I walked in, my phone was ringing. "Rebecca. Roger DeCampo in Seattle." He had a rich, deep voice that I liked at once.

He was divorced, had a kid—pretty generally sounded like an eligible man. I wasn't especially in the market for one; I was dating a very nice marine biologist.

But Julio lived in another town, and we weren't seeing each other exclusively. Since the cosmos had apparently gone to all the trouble of arranging a blind date especially for me, it was the least I could do to accept. I said I'd stay overnight in Seattle and have dinner with him.

It was a lark and it made me giggle, but I certainly wasn't going to meet a strange man at a strange restaurant in a strange city without telling Chris where I was going and with whom.

And far from advising caution, she got right in the spirit of it. "Let's see, you met the friend in the post office, right? So if you marry this dude does that make you a mail-order bride?"

"Listen, do you think it's weird about the three psychics? It kind of gives me the willies."

"Why?"

"Well, three out of three. It's just strange."

"It's strange, all right. They don't call it Berzerkley for nothing."

Roger was about five-nine, skinny, brown hair, brown eyes—nobody's dream boat but certainly not repulsive. And he was interesting. He knew a whole lot about pop culture as well as the more serious subject of Eastern religion, which I've always found fascinating; and he knew about western religion as well. And he was a movie fan who liked country music. A curious combination. A great talker. A good first date.

We got to talking so hard and fast they closed the restaurant down and started stacking chairs before we took the hint and left. And all the time I kept wondering: What are we really doing here? What could possibly be 'important' about the two of us meeting?

Nothing, I thought—just a cute meet, a pleasant time, that was the end of it. But then Roger called and said he'd like to come see me in San Francisco.

What was the harm, I thought?

He took me to Tadich's, an old-fashioned restaurant he'd liked when he visited before. I liked it too, and thought there was a lot to be said for continuity in a city where the half-life of a restaurant is about the time it takes to read the menu.

Roger had by this time become so convinced we were going to be important together that he'd decided to tell me his secrets. He said some things about "new paradigms," for instance, that I didn't begin to get the hang of. I thought perhaps it was a kind of password, a phrase like, "Are you a friend of Bill Wilson?"—an invitation to declare yourself if you're in the club. I didn't, but Roger was undaunted. He went right ahead and told me about his deep and abiding interest in UFOs. He didn't stop there either. He wanted to know what I thought of all that.

I thought it was weird.

But I said it wasn't something I'd thought much about. And then it occurred to me to ask him why he was interested, if he'd ever seen one, or what. I can still remember his exact words.

"Not exactly," he said, "but I've been present at at least three meetings of the Interplanetary Council."

Whereupon I nearly choked on my cioppino.

"Mm—what's that?" I tried to keep my voice casual.

He looked at me seriously. "It's what it sounds like."

"And where were the meetings?"

"They were—well—not in this galaxy."

"But how did you get there? I mean, it's impossible, even traveling at the speed of light."

"You just travel at the speed of thought, that's all."

So there I was, right in Tadich's, as safe and warm a harbor as you can hope to find in this galaxy, talking about the Interplanetary Council. Well, hang on to your hat, I thought; might as well enjoy it. I made the poor man tell me every detail.

Unfortunately, he didn't know too many because he couldn't remember his trips to the other galaxy, he just knew about them because the story was written in the Akashic Records, which, according to him, chronicled everyone's lives, both current and past, from time immemorial. He was *really* vague about where they were, but he did know that they comprised such a huge library that it took ten thousand sentient beings (of who knew what description) to keep track of them. Which didn't strike me as nearly enough if the Interplanetary Council implied what I thought it did.

He knew about all this because he had friends who were in daily contact with extraterrestrials and who lived a kind of shadow existence that shaped life on Earth. The setup reminded me of the premise of *Slaughterhouse Five*, in which, if you recall, a race of aliens called Tralfamadorians control the lives of Earthlings.

Roger described a few potentially earth-shattering disasters his friends had averted by using technologies not dreamed of by most of us, and then he swore me to secrecy on the details. After that, he told me how I fit into all this.

It was the funniest thing, actually. One of his friends, that same person who'd invented some of the futuristic technology, was involved in a legal battle over patents, and I was the lawyer who could get him out of it.

"Oh, gosh," I said, "I'm afraid I couldn't handle something like that on a pro bono basis."

Roger looked absolutely horrified. "It won't be pro bono. Stewart's loaded. It's just that . . . you're the one."

"Why do you say that?"

"I don't. Stewart does. When I got back to Seattle, I told him about the psychics, and he said, 'I already know about her.' "

"How did he know?"

"Stewart knows lots of stuff. You're gonna love this guy—I can't wait for you to meet him."

Somehow, I just wasn't interested.

I still don't know if Stewart is a real person or the imaginary playmate of an adult with a child's imagination. Or if Roger DeCampo has somehow been victimized by a gang of screwballs who've managed to convince him they have daily commerce with extraterrestrials.

Or if, as Chris flatly declared, "He's crazy."

"Well, I'm not so sure. I've called the college where he teaches, and he really does teach there. I've seen pictures of his kids, so they're real. And I even have a book he wrote."

"A published book?" She looked down her ski jump of a nose.

"Uh-huh. A comparison of Eastern religion with Western monotheism. I thought it was good."

"A crazy person could write a book."

"A crazy person isn't supposed to be able to function, and he does that perfectly well. He's very interesting when he's talking about his subject—meaning religion, not UFOs.''

"Look, anybody who sees little green men is out there.''

"But the thing is, he doesn't. Only his friends do.''

"He's a fruitcake, partner. And sometimes I'm not so sure about you.''

"Me?''

"After all, you went on a blind date with somebody recommended by a stranger on the street on the basis of predictions by a psychic.''

"You mean you wouldn't have?''

"Well, certainly not without consulting my own psychic.''

Perhaps it had been a bit rash, and yet I wouldn't have given up the experience. I hadn't known there were people like that, people who seemed utterly normal, who by all accounts led perfectly normal lives, but who operated in a wildly different reality. Yet how was Roger DeCampo any different from a person who believed in the Judeo-Christian god, a concept no more provable than space aliens? The only difference I could see was that the prevailing culture supported one belief system and condemned the other.

But there was no convincing Chris. To her, he was a nut case and that was the end of it. And honestly, I didn't expect to convince her. I knew her, knew how her mind worked—or thought I did until the night she called me from the Hall of Justice.

It was a Thursday night, nearly midnight, and I was snug in my bed, not yet asleep but well on the way. The thing she said, the first thing out of her mouth, was so urban, so typical of her, so nearly brittle: "Listen. Do you believe that she who acts as her own lawyer has a fool for a client?''

I came bolt upright. "Chris, what is it?"

Drunk driving, I thought. She didn't drink that much, but what else could it be?

This was her story:

She'd been driving home, minding her own business, when a police car had stopped her. The officers therein had asked if she was Chris Nicholson, taken a good look at her car, wondered how it got all bent, and brought her down to the Hall of Justice where they'd asked a number of other impertinent questions. She'd made a scene, of course. They finally told her there'd been a hit-and-run a couple of hours before, and a witness had gotten her license number.

At the Hall of Justice, she had been met by our old— I won't say friends—our old acquaintances and rivals, Martinez and Curry of Homicide, who'd given her the notion she was in a heap of shit.

I splashed water on my face, pulled on some clothes, and made it to the Hall in a little over twenty minutes. Thursday night was the worst possible time to get arrested. They could hold Chris for forty-eight hours without charging her, but since there was no court on either Saturday or Sunday, that meant my genteel Southern law partner had an excellent chance of spending three days and four nights in jail.

There was only one solution—she had to talk her way out of it. It was ironic, since "clam up" was the first advice I usually gave anybody, but I desperately wanted Chris to sing like Pavarotti if that meant I could take her home that night. Because of course she had nothing to hide; not Chris.

By the time I got to the Hall, she was the color of instant mashed potatoes, and she was smoking, something I'd never seen her do.

"Since when," I said, "have you been leading a double life?"

She turned a becoming shade of pink. "What?"

"Cigarettes. You're a secret smoker."

"Oh." She laughed nervously. "About three minutes. On the double life." She wasn't at ease, even with me.

"What's going on?" I said when we were alone.

"Jason McKendrick was killed tonight." She shrugged. "They think I did it. I can't seem to talk them out of it."

"Jason McKendrick the critic? Is that who we're talking about?"

"Uh-huh." He worked for the *Chronicle*, reviewed movies, music, and theater, and was more of a celebrity in our town than most people he covered.

"Did you even know him?"

She shook her head. But I thought uneasily about the way she'd blushed when I made the double-life remark.

"Well, why you?"

"Somebody plowed into him in a car that looks like mine, and apparently there was a witness who got the license number just screwed up enough that it came out the same as mine."

"Didn't you say something about your car being bent?"

"Well, yes, I didn't even notice. I guess somebody backed into me in a parking space."

"Was there—you know—blood or hair or anything?"

She turned red again. "I guess they're checking that."

I sat back in my chair.

"Did they give you a blood alcohol test?"

"Just roadside sobriety. Which I passed."

"Did the witness describe the driver of the car?"

She shrugged. "Martinez says so—he says they've got two witnesses. But he could be lying."

"This doesn't look too good."

"It gets worse."

"Tell me."

"The witnesses say it looked like a deliberate hit—the car swerved to hit McKendrick, he tried to dodge it, then it backed up for another try and chased him almost up on the sidewalk. That's why they're handling it like a homicide."

I shrugged. "No big deal. It was clearly the most horrifying thing they ever saw. No wonder they screwed up the license number."

But I was blustering and we both knew it. They had plenty to arrest her on, especially if they found physical evidence on her car. A good alibi could save her in the long run, but they sure weren't going to go checking it out that night.

Desperate, I said, "How are we going to get you out of here?"

"I told them I'd talk after you got here."

"Great. What are you going to say?"

"I was lying. I thought you could talk Martinez into letting me go."

"Oh, sure. He loves me like a daughter." I was impatient with her, couldn't help feeling she didn't understand just how much trouble she was in. "Did they say when McKendrick was killed?"

"About eight-thirty. One of the witnesses called 911."

"Where were you then?"

"At somebody's house."

"Whose? A guy's?"

"No. Someone you don't know."

"Fine. Who?"

"A woman named Rosalie."

"Rosalie who?"

"I don't know her last name."

I didn't say anything, just tried to digest all this, when she said, "I don't know her. I was just . . . at her house."

"Was anybody else there?"

"Yes. Three or four other people."

Oh, God, I was thinking. *Three or four. Which? Three? Four?* Couldn't my law partner count anymore?

This whole deal was crazy. I realized suddenly that I'd been pulling reluctant little factoids out of her as if she were a client referred by a third party—someone I'd never met; and furthermore, someone acting guilty. Someone with a lot to hide from her lawyer.

I said, "Chris, what's going on?"

She looked at me a moment, then stared off into space. She was wearing a white cotton sweater, which didn't help her color any. She was so washed out she was almost ghostly.

Finally she clasped her hands, composing herself, and looked back in my direction. "It's not something I can talk about."

Martinez would have loved to arrest her, and Curry always went along with Martinez. But she'd agreed to a voluntary mug shot, which they'd probably showed to the witnesses, or would in the morning. Either way they didn't have an ID. We figured that out because they let her go.

But if their physical evidence panned out, and if they turned up anything at all that passed for a motive, I was pretty sure they were going to arrest her.

Chris knew it, too. As soon as we got in the car, she said, "Oh, man, am I in trouble. Jesus shit, Rebecca, this is unbelievable."

"Tell me about it." It was partly just a remark and partly a plea.

"You don't know the half of it."

"Whose fault is that?"

"I'm sorry—it's just that I'm going to look guilty as hell. And that's still not the worst of it."

I was getting impatient. "Look, were you having an affair with McKendrick? You know I'm not going to get judgmental about something like that."

"Yeah, but you will about what it actually was."

"Well, just tell me, Chris. Then we'll deal with it."

"You'll never speak to me again."

I decided to let it go. It was a decision that lasted all of two-and-a-half seconds. A horrible notion at the back of my consciousness was inching forward and starting to nag. "Drugs?" I blurted.

She turned toward me. Watching the road, I couldn't see her face, but I felt the indignation that flamed in every cell of her being.

"Of course not. It's nothing illegal, Rebecca."

Just something so shameful she wouldn't even tell her best friend and partner about it.

She didn't talk for the rest of the ride, but she said a strange thing when I dropped her off: "Go see Rosalie. Talk to her and the others. I want you to see what we're up against."

CHAPTER
2

Fortunately, I didn't have to be in court the next morning.

I phoned our secretary, Alan Kruzick, filled him in, told him I wouldn't be in until ten or eleven, and asked him to cancel my one appointment. For once—and I almost gave him a raise for this—he behaved in a businesslike and responsible manner.

It was an odd request Chris had made, to spend the morning chasing strangers. But she was my most important client now, and she must have had a reason, I thought. So eight-thirty found me driving to a rundown building on Larkin Street, very near the Tenderloin. Chris had given me Rosalie's address, but I didn't know if "the others" lived there or somewhere else.

Parking, I thought maybe it was drugs after all—this was the neighborhood for it. I began to wonder if I should have come alone.

But Rosalie didn't look even slightly scary. She seemed to be a trusting soul happy to let someone who claimed to be Chris's lawyer into her apartment. She was in her sixties, I guess, dressed in brown polyester pants and a Kmartish green sweater. Her shoes were thick-soled brown lace-ups, good for hiking—I guessed she probably didn't have a car and did her errands on foot. Her hair was short, brown going gray, and a little thin. It looked a lot as if a neighbor or perhaps her sister had cut it, or maybe she had lost at six-dollar-salon Russian roulette. She was overweight, someone who probably found those errands I imagined adequate for her exercise. She wore no makeup, and most of her appearance suggested she didn't give a damn how she looked, except for one small but attractive bow to feminine adornment—a pair of earrings depicting the goddess Isis.

The Egyptian theme was apparent in some of her furnishings as well, such as a miniature pyramid that may have been a sculpture; I wasn't sure. There was also a black jackal-headed statue, ceramic perhaps, which would have been a little frightening if I hadn't recognized it as the Egyptian god Anubis. The room was furnished with makeshift furniture brightened with ethnic throws, some quite lovely, one or two plain shabby. The beige rug was stained. The bookshelves were bricks and boards, and jam-packed—one or two titles I could see indicated an interest in the occult. And there were plenty of candles, which may have been another indication. On the walls were posters, one for a psychic fair, the other depicting a mermaid or some-such ethereal creature.

It was an unusual room for the neighborhood. Here was a woman who was obviously educated, clearly a nonconformist of some description, and poor. Despite the lack of luxury, I guessed that Rosalie was quite comfortable and cozy here. A hand-thrown teapot with matching cup sat on the coffee table, along with the morning paper, one section open and folded back. The place was clean and got lots of light. It had a nice feel to it—good vibes, positive energy, something of that sort. (The jargon had leapt into my head, making me feel like a New Paradigm woman.)

"I like Chris so much," said Rosalie, when I was sitting on one of her shabby chairs, having refused her offer of tea. "Is she . . . all right?" She had hesitated a moment, caught between curiosity and discretion.

"She's fine, absolutely fine. But there's been a mix-up, and I'm afraid it might develop into a court case. So I'm trying to determine what our chances would be." I was trying hard to make it sound like a civil case, a simple lawsuit. "I was just wondering if I could get your version of what happened last night."

"You mean what happened here? I think you'd better tell me what's going on." She looked a little under fire.

"Oh, no. Nothing to do with what happened here." Damn! I was never going to find out what it was. "The main thing I need to know is when Chris arrived and when she left."

"Well, our meeting was set for eight o'clock, but nobody's ever on time, so I never even bother to look. Let's see, Ivan got here first, and then Moonblood; and Tanesha, finally. It was Chris's first time, and she got lost on the way over—oh, and she had trouble parking. By the time she got here, it might have been after eight-thirty. But I'm not really sure, it could have been a little bit before."

"What kind of meeting was it?"

"Chris didn't tell you?"

"She was kind of shell-shocked."

Rosalie frowned. "I think I'd better talk to the cards."

"I beg your pardon?"

She started to unwrap what looked like a silk scarf she'd scooped up from the top of a bookshelf. It was knotted and contained something fairly heavy. She didn't answer me, just pulled out her Tarot deck and went to work. I sat in amazement as she put on a pair of glasses, shuffled, and laid out cards. When she had made a sort of cross with them she gathered them up without even seeming to pay much attention, certainly not taking time to contemplate, just took them up, nodding to herself.

"You seem okay," she said. "But I think we should leave the content of the meeting out of this. If Chris wants you to know, she'll tell you."

"You read the Tarot?" I asked, rather redundantly.

"Yes."

"I mean . . . um . . . professionally?"

She nodded. "Would you like a reading?"

I looked at my watch. "Thanks, but not right now. I've got to get back to work. When did Chris leave exactly?"

"Exactly isn't my cup of tea, exactly. Ten-thirty, I guess. Something like that. I was too tranced out to notice. Sometimes I get like that—good thing I don't have a car."

"A car?" Why had she mentioned a car if she didn't know what was going on?

"I'd probably be a menace in one." Was she watching me, trying to see if she'd hit a nerve? I decided I was being paranoid.

"I wonder if you could give me the names and addresses of the other people who were here last night."

"I think you should get them from Chris."

"But she told me specifically to see them. Somehow, I got the idea she didn't know their last names."

Rosalie closed her eyes for a minute, scowling almost. Finally she opened them and said, "I think it's best. She's in too much trouble to take this lightly. And we have to move fast."

"How do you know that?"

"I really couldn't tell you." Just those few words and

then a serious clam-up. But she hesitated once again, as if she'd have loved to tell me, actually, but didn't see the point. Maybe she was in touch with some garrulous ETs. I didn't think so, though—I'd never heard of them being invisible.

"Just a second," she said, and disappeared. She came back with a piece of paper that had three names on it, along with addresses and phone numbers: Ivan Shensky; Moonblood Seacrystal; and Tanesha Johnson.

"Do you know where they work?" I said. "I'd like to go see them now."

"Ivan's a night worker. He'll be home. Tanesha works for the Bank of America, in the B. of A. building downtown. Moonblood's a carpenter—you never know where she'll be from one day to the next. Or she might be between jobs. But her roommate's an artist—she's always home; she'd probably be able to point you in the right direction." I tried to imagine what the roommate's name might be. Spiderweb Riverbed Shalecliff Earthnurture? But nothing I thought of surpassed Moonblood Seacrystal—some things just can't be satirized.

Moonblood lived in Noe Valley, and as I drove over, I found myself profoundly uncomfortable. So far I had Chris arriving "about" the time of the murder (if that was what it was). But Chris might have been late—I didn't even know where McKendrick had been killed, how her arrival might fit the time frame.

Next I had a potential witness who couldn't be bothered looking at clocks, who consorted with people named Moonblood, who got too "tranced out" to notice little things like arrivals and departures, and who closed her eyes and screwed up her face before answering certain questions—that is, if she didn't whip out a Tarot deck. I had to hope at least one of the three others

at the "meeting" would show up a little better in court.
And if that person was Moonblood, I had to hope she
had a nickname.

Moonblood lived in a cottage behind a larger house,
a dollhouse almost, barely big enough for one, much
less two and canvases. The yard was beautifully kept,
boasting an elaborate herb border, flagstones, even a
hammock. A lot of love and effort had gone into it,
which boded well, I thought. A completely crazy person couldn't have designed it. Folk music of some sort,
guitars and women's voices, blared from the cottage. I
was about to knock on the newly painted dark green
door when a voice behind me said, "Can I help you?"

The woman behind me was short and compact, wearing overalls over a T-shirt. She had biceps that looked
as if they'd driven many a nail, and a buzz haircut with
a minute semblance of a curl over one eye—something
like James Bond's comma of black hair except that it
was light brown and too short to punctuate a sentence.
She was somewhere in her thirties, I thought.

"Are you Moonblood Seacrystal?" I hoped I was
keeping a straight face.

"You got a problem with that?"

"A problem? No, I just . . . I mean, I don't even
know you."

"I meant my name."

"Mine's Rebecca Schwartz," I said, and stuck out
my hand, which she ignored. "I'm here about my law
partner, Chris Nicholson."

"Don't know him."

"It's a woman. I think you were with her last night.
On Larkin Street, at Rosalie's." Damn. I'd been so flustered I hadn't even gotten Rosalie's last name.

"Oh, Chris. The new kid. Has something happened
to her?"

"Well, in a way. The police think she was involved in an accident on her way to Rosalie's. I'm wondering if you can remember what time she got there."

"I don't know. She was already there when I arrived."

"What time was that?"

She shrugged. "About eight-twenty, maybe. Who knows?"

I felt little drops of sweat pop out at my hairline. "It could be important."

She held up her left arm, which was bare at the wrist. "Do you see a watch? I don't know what I don't know."

"Rosalie said Chris got to her house last."

"Oh, Rosalie. She's brilliant, but crazy. Chris was there when I got there. I'd never seen her before. How was I not going to notice someone who looks like Big Bird?"

I was deeply offended. Chris is six feet tall and does have a long nose, but she also has long fingers and long legs—everything about her is long, and in fact, she's quite elegant. Only a truly mean-spirited person could describe her as looking like Big Bird. Having had quite enough of Moonblood Seacrystal, I left in a huff.

It was a huff brought on not only by the Big Bird remark, but by frustration born of fear—so far Chris didn't begin to have an alibi. If Martinez started interviewing these characters, he was going to think he'd ended up in Conviction Heaven.

But maybe he wouldn't. No doubt the witnesses were wrong about the plate, and there wasn't going to be any evidence on Chris's car. Everything would be fine. I decided it had been noble of me to go knocking on doors first thing in the morning but probably precipitous. I'd just call the office and see how things were going.

"Alan; give me Chris."

"She's not coming in till after lunch. What's going on with you two, anyway? I've been so busy canceling appointments I haven't had time to do my nails, let alone watch the soaps."

"Has anyone a wee bit unusual dropped by?"

"Funny you should ask. Those cop friends of yours—Martinez and Curry—were here asking for Chris. Just left, matter of fact."

Quickly I called Chris. "Listen, you might want to make yourself scarce. Kruzick says Martinez and Curry are looking for you. You probably have about fifteen minutes to get out of there."

"I'm out of here, but could we get together this afternoon? I'm fed up with this shit."

"What shit?"

"My goddamn secret life."

I tried to keep my voice level, as if she said that sort of thing all the time. "Actually, I have afternoon appointments—how about lunch?"

"Great."

We agreed on one o'clock, and I went off to see Ivan Shensky.

I probably shouldn't have, I guess—Rosalie had told me he was a night worker—but I had no mercy where Chris was concerned. Shensky lived on Twin Peaks, in a flavorless, colorless apartment building with a fabulous view no doubt, but I never got to see it. On about the nineteenth ring of his bell, he ambled down to see what manner of sadist had come calling.

His hair was rumpled; he'd pulled on a pair of Chi pants and a T-shirt.

"I'm really sorry," I began, not wanting to give him a chance to yell at me, but he didn't seem angry, merely puzzled. "I wouldn't have come unless it was as important as it is. I'm Chris Nicholson's attorney and—"

"Who?"

"Chris Nicholson. From the group at Rosalie's."

"Oh, yeah. Raiders of the Lost Art."

"I beg your pardon?"

"Sure. Tall woman. Looks like a model."

"Thank you for that."

"What? Are you her mother or something?"

"I meant for the confirmation. I just talked to another member of your group who made an unkind remark about her."

"Oh, Moonblood. She'd be a lot happier if she'd just call herself Susie or Kathy or something. She's so busy being defensive about her name she's got a permanent chip on the shoulder."

I liked Ivan. Not only wasn't he mad at me for getting him out of bed, but he seemed a kind-hearted person. He was a shortish guy, and slight, with narrow shoulders and a narrow face, somewhat dark and slightly pensive; short hair, cute moustache. A thoroughly decent sort.

So imagine my surprise when he said, "God, I'd love to get my hands on you." And turned immediately scarlet.

"What?"

"Oh God, I blurted again. I'm going to lose another job if I don't stop that. I meant, I can see your back hurts from those high heels you're wearing. I just thought . . . I thought I could help you."

"Are you a body worker or something?"

"An RN, actually. But that wasn't what I meant. I know a little about pressure points." He shrugged. "It wasn't a come-on or anything."

Of course not. "Look, a legal problem has come up.

I wonder if you can tell me what time Chris arrived and left last night."

"I don't think I should answer questions like that without talking to Chris. I mean, you might not be her lawyer—maybe you're a jealous wife who thinks she's dallying with your husband. You seem like a very nice person, but what if—"

I put up a hand. "I understand. Look, I'll have her phone you if it becomes important."

He breathed in, obviously relieved. "Thanks for understanding. Listen, if you want—I really could work on your back. You want to turn around a minute?"

I got out of there as fast as I could. But I kicked off those shoes the minute I was in my car. I'd found them on a half-price sale and bought them even though they didn't fit right. My back did hurt, but I wouldn't have thought it was so obvious. I wondered if I was developing bad posture.

And once again I wondered what sort of rat's nest Chris had gotten herself into. Spiffed up in a suit, Shensky might at least look acceptable to a jury, but there was that habit he had of "blurting." What was his problem? And more to the point, what was Chris doing with a group called Raiders of the Lost Art?

Tanesha Johnson wasn't about to tell me. When I finally found her office—after a few fits, starts, and long conversations with the guard—I was delighted to see a well-groomed young black woman, decked out in full makeup, sporting a fresh manicure, with a nameplate on her desk saying she was my quarry. Now this one I could take to court. I handed her my card. "Ms. Johnson? I'm Rebecca Schwartz. I'm here about Chris Nicholson from Raiders of the Lost Art. . . ."

Her neck swiveled, and as there were two other people in the reception room over which she presided, her voice dropped to a hiss. "What the hell do you mean coming here like this?"

Taken aback, I said, "A legal problem has come up and I had a question—"

"Lady, you're jeopardizing my job, do you know that?"

So that was number four. I could hardly wait for lunch, and not because I was hungry. But I would have waited a week to eat if it meant not seeing the wreck of my confident, competent law partner. She was wearing jeans and a pair of shades, which she removed to show a face splotchy with crying; she was shaking.

"Rebecca, I think they're going to arrest me."

CHAPTER 3

We'd met at a dim sum place, her favorite, and to get her calmed down, I resorted to my mother's tricks, the infamous behavior of the females of my tribe. I begged her to eat; I cajoled her with dainty morsels. She was so distracted, trying to get something down to get me off her back that she forgot to cry for a while.

And finally I had the nerve to open the subject. "So about the secret life."

She looked as if I'd kicked her. For a full thirty seconds she stared at me full in the face, brow furrowed. At the time I thought she was furious, but in retrospect I realized she'd been trying to figure out what on earth to say. The things that whizzed through my head ran the gamut from gunrunning to black magic—with a bias, owing to the name of the group and Moonblood's hostility, toward the latter.

In the end she opted for simplicity, a two-word statement that said it all—and left me thoroughly puzzled: "I'm psychic."

I almost laughed, I was so relieved. How wonderful that she wasn't running a child-stealing ring! "Oh, is that all."

"All? What do you mean 'all'? Rebecca, have you forgotten you think psychics are bunk? I'm not a credible person anymore.'' She snapped her fingers. ''Just like that—a lifetime of rationality. Gone. Wiped out.''

I didn't know if she meant mine or hers. Mine was ebbing fast. Okay, it was gone by the time I grasped what she'd said: Chris wouldn't lie to me. Therefore she was psychic.

If a rational person couldn't believe in psychics, then I no longer was one. But I was still about a million miles from having any idea what was going on. I proceeded with caution.

''What, exactly, does being psychic mean? I mean, to you.''

''Good God, Rebecca—if you can't do any better in court, I'm going to the Big House.''

''Wait a minute—this is just you and me. Can't we . . .'' I realized what I wanted and said it, ''. . . be friends?''

''What?''

''You're so defensive you're putting miles between us. How about just pretending I'm not going to kill you if you tell me? I know it's asking a lot, but we've known each other six or eight years now, and I haven't killed you yet. Not even when you let my mom talk you into talking me into hiring Kruzick.''

She almost laughed, I could see her face muscles hovering.

''And *that* was a killing offense,'' I said.

''I don't know how to talk about this stuff.''

''How about if I ask questions?''

''I don't know how to answer them.''

''Well, just say something, okay? Pretend your life isn't hanging in the balance. We're just two pals exchanging girlish confidences.''

She stared at the battered table between us. ''It started when I was a kid.''

I felt hurt that this had been such a big part of her life and she'd kept it from me so thoroughly.

"I saw things I wasn't supposed to see—you know what I mean?"

I shook my head.

"Well, I started crying once and caused a big family stink because my Uncle Wade and Aunt Tootie were getting divorced. Only nobody knew it yet, including Aunt Tootie. Wade had a sweetie he finally married.

"And one other thing—don't lose your lunch, please—I saw auras."

"What!" It was a statement of outrage, not a question. Only screwballs saw auras; auras didn't exist. I pulled it together enough to ask what they looked like.

"Light around people," she said. "Different-colored light. My mom would say, 'Do you want to go play with Janet today?' And I'd say, 'I don't like Janet. She's green.' Now tell me something. What do you think was the reaction of my family?"

"They told you there was no such thing, it must be your imagination."

"At first, yes. After awhile I got punished for it. And of course I never knew what was going to get me in trouble because I didn't know what I saw that nobody else saw. Sometimes I saw people—and sometimes they were in period costume, so I'd say, 'Daddy, why is that man all dressed up like George Washington?' And he'd say, 'there's no man over there, Chris. If you don't stop telling these stories you're going to bed without supper.' So gradually, I can't say how any more than I can say how a child learns to speak, I learned to tune it out. I got so I only saw the stuff everybody else did—when I was nine or ten, I guess." She looked up at me, defeated. "And it didn't come back until three or four years ago."

"What happened?"

"I started seeing things. I started seeing colors where there weren't any, and surrealistic visions that came out of nowhere. Remember that time I took a week off and didn't say exactly why?"

"Yes. I thought you were just stressed out."

"Well, believe me, I was. But it wasn't the usual kind of stress. I thought I was going crazy. I really did. I was so depressed I felt like packing it in."

"Chris!"

"Oh, I wasn't suicidal. Just so scared and depressed and so miserable I was starting to wish I was. And I couldn't bring myself to make an appointment with a shrink. I guess I was afraid of getting the bad news. I was basically just planning to lie around and try to figure out what to do.

"But I got up and went to a coffeehouse one day, and while I was sitting there all forlorn with my cappuccino, I picked up one of those free magazines that list all the weird stuff you can do—you know those things? Seminars on how to meet your ideal mate and classes in prestidigitation? Well, there was a whole section on psychics, and there was this one who would do a phone reading and put it on your credit card. I'd never have done it if I actually had to get up the energy to make an appointment, but, you know, all you had to do was dial. I don't know why, I just did it."

My head was reeling at the strangeness of it all, but this part sounded familiar. When I'm about as far down in the dumps as you can get, I can't resist reading my horoscope in every magazine at the supermarket. It's not that I expect any of them to be right—I just want a moment's flash of hope: "Look for money when the moon goes into Aries; harmony will return to your house after the 24th."

"She started out by saying, 'You're really depressed, aren't you?' And then she said, 'There's something you don't understand in your life.' And she said a few innocuous things that sailed on past me, and then she just said, flat out, 'Look, I've got to stop the reading and just talk to you. The same thing's happening to you that happened to me. Tell me something, are you aware of your psychic abilities?' Can you imagine? I nearly hung up."

I laughed, putting myself in her place, at my wit's end with a crackpot on the phone. "What'd you say?"

"I said no, I wasn't. Rebecca, I'd completely forgotten what happened to me as a kid. Or at any rate, I didn't connect it with being psychic—it was just some strange thing that I managed to outgrow. She said, 'Are you seeing things that aren't there? Hearing voices? Anything like that?' And when she said it, I was so grateful I wasn't hearing voices I sat down on the floor and started crying. She said it happened to her, the whole thing, and she actually went to a shrink who gave her drugs that turned it off pretty well until she did the same thing I did—happened on a psychic who knew what it was. And then she told me it was curable."

"Wait a minute. You mean you aren't psychic after all?"

"The craziness, the randomness is curable. It's like anything else, you just have to learn what to do with it. You know how kids start out making random sounds? And then they finally say, 'I keem,' and their parents say 'ice cream,' Rebecca. Say 'ice.' Okay now, 'cream.' Psychic focusing is a skill that can be taught. It's a whole little science, and that's what psychic readers are all about—they're people who've learned to tune in to their intuition."

You don't believe that, I wanted to say. *You can't.*

You're a rational person in business with me. Psychic readers are charlatans.

"You make it sound like anybody can do it."

"They say anybody can. But something tells me it would take a lot more work if you weren't already out there like I was."

"You signed up for the course, I take it."

"That one and a few more. Sanity restored—praise the lord and pass the ammunition. All's well on the Western front." She stopped and ate a potsticker. "There's only one thing. When you have something like this—I hesitate to call it a gift—it nags at you."

My ex-boyfriend Rob has a close friend who writes fiction and who describes a similar syndrome.

She shrugged. "Hence the Raiders of the Lost Art."

"Wait a second, you lost me."

"Well, we were all doing this kind of work, and we happened to meet—I don't know, at different workshops and things. There's a whole culture around this, you know."

I did know. You couldn't live in the Bay Area and not know. The Psychic Fair, for instance, attracted thousands of people every time they had it—maybe hundreds of thousands. But the idea of Chris among the crystal-wearers just about broke my heart. Why? I wondered.

Because I felt betrayed. Lied to. Left out.

She polished off a shrimp and mushroom dumpling. "Well, actually we didn't all know each other till Rosalie got us together. I've known Tanesha forever. Rosalie was my teacher once, and also hers—I lied at the police station. You know when I said I didn't know her? I'm sorry, I just . . ." She let it tail off, letting me fill in the blank: "I didn't want to admit I did."

"So she's really the center of the group; she asked the four of us to join about three months ago."

"Wait a minute. If she was your teacher, why don't you know her last name? Or were you just withholding it?"

"She doesn't use it. None of us do much. I mean I know Tanesha's, and Rosalie knows everybody's, I guess, but it's a weird world—you don't necessarily want people to know that much about you."

I nodded. "Okay, go on."

"Well, at first I didn't want to join the group. And then, about a week ago, I just felt a desperate need to do it. I knew I couldn't leave it alone; I really needed to work with other people." She stopped and stared at me a moment, obviously trying to decide whether she should continue. Finally she said, "I really wanted to push the edges of the envelope."

"Just what are you doing in there?"

"Oh, different things. Last night was my first meeting, you know. But I think they've been doing a lot of group readings; and Moonblood wants to try predicting the lottery numbers, but I was in a group once that worked on horseracing, and we didn't have any luck at all. The future is far and away the hardest part—hardly anybody ever gets it right, which is probably what makes most people think we're a bunch of charlatans. Because that's what everybody wants to know about, and so the temptation is to try to tell them. But we're usually wrong." She stopped again, getting to the hard stuff. "And then, there's some stuff we do that's a little harder to describe."

"Like what?" I couldn't help myself.

"You really want to know?"

"Umm. Maybe later." Maybe this was enough for now.

She had been animated when she was telling about her secret life, as she called it, but the fear took over again.

"It's the same as not having an alibi, you know what I mean? Martinez and Curry are going to interview those people and decide they're a bunch of weirdos that no jury would believe."

"Tanesha seems all right."

"Tanesha's so terrified someone's going to find out about her you'd think she was a Commie in the McCarthy era. You think she's going to get up on the witness stand and say she was with me, trying to contact the ghost of Christmas past? More likely she'd say she's never seen me before in her life. Ivan's okay—in fact he's really got the most interesting story of all—except that he got fired once for trying to do psychic healing on a patient. Just doing it wouldn't have been so bad, but the patient hadn't asked for it. He sees trouble spots on people's bodies, and he just wants to go for them."

"I don't see why that would come up in court."

She shook her head vigorously. "Ivan blurts stuff. He's very young, I guess, I don't know. No way I'd let him testify for me. You just couldn't trust him. And then there's Rosalie, who pretty much speaks her own language; and Moonblood's name alone would make half the jury laugh and the other half throw up. Besides, Rebecca, here's the thing—we were all in deep trance last night. If that came out, which it's bound to, nobody'd believe a word any of us said."

I thought about the way Martinez and Curry would think; all they wanted was to make a case. She was right—the alibi she had was like none at all. And, assuming she got off, if being accused of murder didn't wreck her career, becoming a known psychic—read flake—most assuredly would.

I was defeated. "Okay. The odds are against us. Let's talk strategy."

"Well, I've been thinking about it. If they're so sure I did it, they're busy checking out my alibi, trying to find a motive, all that stuff, right? But of course you and I know they're barking up the wrong tree. The real question is who did kill McKendrick."

"You're psychic. You tell me."

She gave me a pained look. "It doesn't work that way."

Well, why the hell didn't it? I made up my mind to ask, eventually, but for now I couldn't afford to get distracted.

"Ladies," said a voice from my past, "if I may make so bold, who killed McKendrick is only the first question."

Our heads swiveled to behold Mr. Rob Burns, my ex-boyfriend, who was standing at the end of our booth, where he'd apparently been eavesdropping on us.

He put up a placating hand. "I only heard the tail end. Really. I just got here."

"To what do we owe the honor?" I asked as coldly as I could.

"I just came from your office, where, incidentally, I observed Inspectors Curry and Martinez. I convinced Alan I could help, so he sent me over."

A million questions pushed to the forefront of my brain, but I hit him with the most immediate. "How do you know they didn't follow you?"

"You think Kruzick and I are amateurs?" He sat down across from me, nudging Chris toward the other end of the booth, suffering not a second's conscience. Rob is a reporter for the *San Francisco Chronicle*. Chutzpah is a requirement for the job.

The next question popped out: "How'd you find out what's happening?"

"I work for the *Chronicle*, remember? The same as Jason McKendrick did; he was a friend of mine."

"Oh, Rob, I'm sorry. I never knew that."

"Well, he wasn't the kind of friend I saw outside the office. Or he wasn't by the time I met you. Jason had a lot of enthusiasms—one after the other."

"He had fights with people?"

"No, he just got tired of them—and it's to his credit that he never seemed to make anybody mad. A very popular guy, Jason. Brilliant. Very complex. He was hard to know, but not at all hard to like. It wouldn't be far off the mark to say that everybody loved him." Nobody mentioned the obvious. "Did you know him, Chris?"

Chris never looked so much like a racehorse— aristocratic and powerful, tightly wound, dangerous— as when she was angry. Her nostrils quivered. I half expected her to toss her head like Silky Sullivan. "Rob, you're pissing me off."

He backed off—literally—turned toward her, and slid his butt toward the end of the booth. But he never lost eye contact. "You're in trouble, Ms. Nicholson. Those idiots at the cop shop want to try to hang it on you. Would it interest you to learn the coroner found a piece of paper with your name and address on it in McKendrick's shirt pocket?"

"What!"

"I thought so. You think Alan told me where you are because I want to help them? Trust me, okay?"

She rolled her eyes. "Oh, sure. I'd be a fool not to." But she laughed. That was something she hadn't done lately.

"Listen, the *Chronicle*'s pulling out all the stops on

this one. Jason was one of our own. I'm assigned to the story, but it's been made clear to me that it isn't only a story—we're out to get the bastard who did this." Though we didn't protest, he held up a placating hand. "A little conflict there, but we're only human. Corporately human, I mean. When I found out you're the number-one suspect, I made a deal with city desk. Someone else is covering the police story, and if you tell me anything that gives me the slightest bit of hope, I'm doing my own investigation. With the blessing of the powers that be, I might add."

Chris sat straight, and she was at least two inches taller than Rob. She spoke in staccato sentences, the way I'd seen her do in court: "I never met the man. I didn't kill him. I appreciate your confidence."

"Good. Then let's work together on this."

"Why should we?" I asked. "I don't mean to be rude, but that's a serious question. What's in it for us, and what's in it for you?"

"I have access to things you need—that little piece of information I just gave you, for instance. And Jason McKendrick's Rolodex, for another thing (Xeroxed, of course—the cops probably have the original by now.). Would you find that useful?"

"We certainly would. And what can we do for you?"

Chris blurted, "Am I in it?"

Rob smiled. "If you had been, the cops wouldn't have got the original." He was a charmer, and he knew Chris well, but I didn't quite believe it; I thought it more likely he didn't suspect her because he hadn't found her name there. He turned to me. "As for what you have that I want, it's information, of course. You have the one piece I need."

"And what's that?" I asked.

The name of the person or persons who'd most like to frame you.''

"I can't think of anybody," said Chris disconsolately. "Everybody fuckin' loves me."

Rob mentioned the obvious: "Not exactly everybody. Look. Even if you don't think you know, you know. We just have to be patient and let it surface."

"I don't get this. Rosalie says I don't have any enemies."

"Goddammit, Chris, how *does* this stuff work? How could she know that?"

Rob looked confused.

"I'm just letting off steam," she said. "It's not the most reliable thing in the world. Obviously I have an enemy."

"Where were you parked?" I asked.

"A couple of blocks from Rosalie's—I had trouble finding a space."

"So somebody must have followed you, stolen your car, and deliberately used it to kill McKendrick. Who they happened to know had your name and address in his pocket."

It was a truly malevolent thing to do, to plan so carefully, snare her so thoroughly. Somebody had it in for her in a big way. And it had to be someone who also wanted to kill McKendrick. Suddenly I had an idea: "I know. I've got it."

"You've got it?"

"Look, he was a critic, right? It was probably somebody whose career he ruined—somebody who didn't even know him."

"Why do you say that?"

"Because what have you and McKendrick got in common? You also get your name in the paper occasionally and also have a job that could be perceived as giving you the power to destroy people. Maybe it was someone you went up against in court who wasn't all that stable. So he decided to kill McKendrick and frame you for it.''

Both Chris and Rob looked excited.

''The down side is, it means you have to look at everything McKendrick ever wrote and see if you recognize any names.''

''It beats being a convicted psychic.'' She glanced at Rob uneasily, but he didn't seem to be listening; he had other things on his mind.

''So what do you think?'' he said. ''About working with me. Think of the money you'll save.''

''How's that?''

''You won't have to hire an investigator.''

I said: ''Your call, Chris.''

''He's got conflicts right and left.''

I assumed the lawyer role: ''What about it, Rob?''

He spread his hands, all innocence. ''Well, technically I do, but who cares about technically? What I want is a story, and you two look like the quickest way to it. There's no conflict there.''

I knew Rob as well as I knew Chris, and six words he had just spoken summed up his whole personality, indeed his *raison d'etre* (and incidentally, the main reason we were no longer together): ''What I want is a story.''

Nothing could be truer. But would he sell us out to get it?

I said: ''You have to promise you won't withhold stuff.''

''Done.''

''I mean really, really promise, Rob. This is Chris's life we're talking about. You have to give us any information relating to the case exactly as if we were paying you.''

''No problem. I swear to God, no problem. As long as you promise not to pass it to the *Ex*.'' The *Examiner*.

Chris nodded, looking pleased. ''I think we've got a deal.''

I'd loved Rob for a long time, and in some ways I was sure I'd love him the rest of my life. And I trusted him, sometimes. But I knew him too well to be completely happy. We needed the Rolodex, and certain other inside info I'd been planning to hit him for anyway—but now I couldn't unless we made the deal. I wanted it, too—with one little refinement. ''There's just one thing. Whenever possible, we really work together—I go with you on interviews, all that sort of thing.''

To my amazement, a look of pure delight started at his mouth and, as the notion sunk in, spread out over his features. ''Sure,'' he said. And for the first time I caught on that he might be motivated by something more than journalistic aggression.

But on the surface, he was all business. ''Chris, I'd like to take you to the *Chron* right away to look at clips. And I need to fill you both in on some things I know from the office.

''First of all, McKendrick was a serious ladies' man—by which I don't mean a philanderer, though he may have been that too. What I mean is someone who spent a lot of time dating. Think about it—he had to go out nearly every night to review something, he always had free tickets, and he was kind of a famous guy, a man about town. It was a great way to get dates and he had plenty of them. Always with good-looking, sophisticated ladies.''

''So maybe we should go and see some of them?''

''Eventually, maybe. But first things first.''

"What do you mean?"

"The woman he lived with. And thereby hangs a tale."

I raised an eyebrow. "Couldn't miss."

"His assistant is a young woman named Adrienne. Real young—twenty-two or -three, maybe. McKendrick was in his late thirties and pretty much dated women that age or older. Sophisticated women, as I said. Very slick articles. Adrienne is a punk in more than one way. Big on attitude. Stupid-looking hairdo, black clothes and eye makeup. Cute in a junior highish kind of way. But definitely not McKendrick's type—in fact, it's kind of weird he even hired her as his assistant. But that I can kind of see if I really stretch things—she gives the impression of hipness, which didn't hurt his image any, and she's got a mouth on her that had to be useful for getting rid of supplicants. Of whom there were hundreds, as you can imagine. Anyway, I thought I'd go talk to her outside the office, so I got her address from the payroll files, and guess what?"

But he'd already given us the punchline. I said, "It was the same as McKendrick's."

He nodded.

"Okay, let's catch her tonight. What about right after work?"

He nodded again, looking so satisfied I don't think the word "smug" would be amiss.

CHAPTER 4

There was nothing to do at that point but face Curry and Martinez. I phoned first and discovered that by that time there was only Curry, which sounded like a good sign and was. Rosalie had refused to give him the names of the three other Raiders without Chris's permission, and so Curry was there to get it—not to read Chris her rights. I could have supplied the names, but did I? Ha. I made a big show of phoning Rosalie and telling her it was fine with us to give the nice police inspector their names and addresses—in fact, I said, we encouraged it. Fortunately, since she had the grace not to answer the phone, I delivered the information by mechanical means and could only hope she'd gone to spend a few days in the country.

Kruzick, forced into uncharacteristic mildness with the heat on the premises, started doing little Columbo bits the second we were alone. If it weren't for Nicholson and Schwartz, the term ''unemployed actor'' would have perfectly described Kruzick and—too bad for the rest of us—to him all the world was a stage. He didn't communicate, he did bits. I would have fired him except that he was my sister Mickey's boyfriend and my mom would have killed me. That day I went in my office and closed the door.

I had two clients to see that afternoon and lots of

paperwork to do, but none of that kept me from turning over and over in my mind what was for me the strangest part of the whole deal—Chris's metaphysical confession. She had been so sad while she was speaking, and so focused, that she hadn't once forgotten anyone's name. Usually, she did that. She got overexuberant and talked too fast and ended up saying "Pigball" or "Whizbang" rather than stop long enough to retrieve the name from her memory bank. The exuberant, excitable Chris hadn't been there at all. True, she was in big, bad trouble, but I sensed it was more than that— she was worried about driving a wedge between us by telling all, maybe irreparably damaging the friendship.

I couldn't say it was in perfect shape. She *had* driven a wedge, though possibly by her secrecy rather than her confession. Yet I couldn't blame her. It wasn't the sort of thing you wanted to get around. It would take me awhile to assimilate it—not only the feelings of betrayal, the changes in Chris, but the notion of "psychic" as something real rather than a close cousin to stage magic. I didn't know it then, on that worried afternoon just trying to get through, but over the next few days my entire world view would change, would shift as a result of what I knew now, and would never return to "normal" again. It was like a loss of innocence.

Rob picked me up at the office, having left just after Adrienne did. Our plan was to call on her immediately, before she had time to go out for the evening.

"How's Chris doing?" I asked. "Did she find anything?"

"Not yet."

He had settled her in the library with miles of microfilm of Jason McKendrick's reviews.

Jason and Adrienne lived on California Street, a few

blocks west of Nob Hill, in a neighborhood that didn't thrill me. If the truth be told, it wasn't that far from where Rosalie lived, and it was about as rundown.

Adrienne spoke through the intercom: "Who is it?"

"Rob Burns. I need to talk to you about Jason."

A sound that was probably a sob came out of her throat, and she buzzed us in.

She must have had time to change after work because she wasn't wearing black. She had pulled a bleached-out pink T-shirt over a pair of white pants that fit like skin and resembled nothing so much as thermal underwear. She hadn't bothered with shoes, and her hairdo, which owed its sassy panache to usually defiant spikes, had started to droop.

The room itself was absolutely astonishing—that is, if you considered that two adults lived there, one nearly forty and well established, the other making at least union wages. All four walls were lined with orange crates and bricks and boards containing books and re-cords—many of them old records, the real thing instead of CDs. There was a mattress on the floor with some rumpled sheets and a pancake of a pillow on it, and one ancient rocking chair with a broken cane seat. There was also an old but expensive stereo set and a CD player. An old crook-necked desk lamp had been plugged in near the mattress. Other than that, there was no furniture. The walls, what few patches you could see of them, had been painted black. It looked like the abode of college students—or possibly of someone Adrienne's age who hadn't grown up yet. But if it had been Adrienne's apart-ment originally—rather than Jason's—what was she doing with the old-fashioned records?

Rob said, "Rebecca Schwartz, Adrienne Dunson." But Adrienne ignored me. She stared at Rob, lower lip trembling. She wanted him to take her in his arms, and he didn't want to. Finally, I gave him a nudge. He didn't step forward, but he opened his arms, and she took the cue. Once she was enfolded, he did fine, patting and cooing as if he were the father of five. While no one was looking, I took a spin around the apartment.

There was a dark, underfurnished kitchen, the walls thick with grime, dishes piled in the sink. Paint peeled from a small table pushed against a wall, but no one ever ate there, I was sure. It was piled a foot high with newspapers, catalogs, magazines, and unopened junk mail. Two chairs that didn't match were drawn up to it.

An inhospitable hall opened onto a bedroom and bath, the bath divided into water closet and shower, in the old San Francisco manner. Both were dirty and dim.

The bedroom was shocking—a piece of fabric, a Cost Plus bedspread from the looks of it, had been tacked over the window to serve as a curtain, so that the room was plunged in perennial darkness. A perfectly plain double bed, unmade, the sheets redolent, was crowded into a corner, clothes littered the floor, and a chipped, white-painted chest of drawers stood against one wall. If I had to guess I would have said depressed people lived there. I'd been on the premises two minutes, and already I felt like eating my gun.

I went in the water closet and flushed the toilet, to cover my spy mission. When I got back, Rob was still holding Adrienne and stroking her hair, but she had stopped crying. "I don't think you should stay here," he was saying.

"I'm fine. Really."

"Where are you from, Adrienne? Do you have relatives around here?"

"I grew up in El Cerrito. Why?"

"Wouldn't you like us to drive you over there? I get the feeling you could use some home cooking."

"My mom's dead."

He gave me a look that said, Help!

I came up behind her and touched her back. "Does your dad still live there? Wouldn't you like to go home for a while?"

Miserably, she shook her head, leaning into Rob, trying to bury her face even deeper into his shoulder. He gripped her upper arms and stepped away from her. "Look at me, honey. Listen, I really don't think you should stay here."

She looked around doubtfully. "I guess . . . Danno . . . I don't know."

"Who's Danno?"

"A guy I used to hang with. But he might not want me there."

"What about a girlfriend?" I said.

She didn't answer, just shook her head to let me know what a dumb idea that was. Either she didn't have any girlfriends or didn't want to stay with one.

"Danno then." I wasn't exactly brimming with sympathy for Adrienne. Her boyfriend was dead and she had a horrible apartment, but on the other hand she didn't seem to be doing a lot to get through the gloom. I know that this is the way with depressed people, but it makes me impatient.

She pulled away from Rob and looked at me, possibly drawn by the edge my voice was developing. "No, I don't think so. I think I should stay here."

The idea sounded dreadful. If the apartment wasn't bad enough, aesthetically speaking, there was the problem of Jason's memory, his clothes scattered on the floor, his toothbrush in the bathroom. I made my voice softer. "You need to be away from Jason. It's so sad this way."

To my surprise, she nodded. "He was killed here,

you know. Right outside—crossing the street on the way to his car. I keep looking out the window. Something draws me there. It's creepy."

I had an almost irresistible urge to look out the window; Rob crossed over and did it. "Isn't that his car?"

She joined him and so did I. "Yeah, it's still there."

Rob pointed it out. "The old Nissan." It was old and battered indeed—far from the sharp little sports car I'd have picked for someone like Jason.

I was thinking how different people can be from their public personas when Adrienne said, "Maybe I *could* go to my dad's. I could stay in my old room and act like a hermit."

I nodded. "Good. We'll take you."

"But it's so quiet there."

I looked around. It had to be better than this.

Rob and I waited while she packed a few things, pulling clothes out of a vanity in the bathroom—an odd place to keep them, but nothing about the household seemed ordinary. And then we drove her across the Bay, me in the backseat, Adrienne next to Rob.

"I'm assigned to the murder story," said Rob. "I guess you know that."

"Murder. Jeez! It's so fucking hard to believe."

"I was wondering if you know of anybody who was mad at him; you know, had a grudge, anything like that."

Slowly, she shook her head. "The police asked me that, and I really can't think of anyone. I mean, people threatened to get him fired all the time, but that was just business as usual. It was just a *thing*. You know, after a bad review. A day or two of temper tantrums, and that was that."

"Really? Because if anyone would know, you would.

You must have been the person closest to him in the world."

She shrugged, her face angry. "I don't know if he was close to anyone."

"But you were his girlfriend and his assistant. You can't get much closer than that."

She turned toward him abruptly. "I wasn't his girlfriend."

"But . . ."

"Oh God, no. Do I look like his type? He was just letting me stay at his place for a while. I mean, after I broke up with Danno, I didn't have any place to go."

"Well, I'm glad to hear that. I thought he was cheating on you with all those other women." He paused, made the next question casual. "Who has he been dating, by the way?"

"Oh, *Jason*. He always had a million women. Usually one at a time, though. Lately, I guess, Felicity Wainwright was the most usual. She's an oncologist. Weird, huh? But I think he was about to dump her. He was starting to have lunch with Sabrina Gelderman. That was usually how he started out. But women called him all the time, you know. He had a ton and a half of them."

"Always dangerous," I said. "If he dated them, he must have dumped them—at least some of them."

She shrugged. "They never seemed to get mad. But then, he did have a little secret."

"What?" Rob and I spoke together.

"Oh, it's just something I think. I can't prove it or anything."

"But what?" A reporter never gives up.

"Just talk to Felicity, why don't you. And maybe Vanda Ragusin—she was right before Felicity."

''Ms. Ragusin didn't get mad when she got dumped?''

''I don't know. It was like the people he reviewed. For a day or two, maybe. Yeah, she might of called up a couple of times and left snitty messages.'' She turned up a palm. ''But that was about it.''

Rob said, ''He must have been a pretty smooth guy. I'd be pretty pissed if someone dumped me.''

Maybe he was trying to tell me something. I had dumped him—he'd found out when he saw my picture in the paper with someone else—but he hadn't seemed even slightly pissed about it. Which, of course, was one of the reasons he needed dumping. Mr. Passion.

Before we dropped Adrienne off, we extracted more names from her—those of Jason's closest men friends and couple friends; there were no women friends, she insisted, even herself.

It was early yet, and I had a date with Julio, the man Rob thinks I dumped him for (though of course it wasn't like that), but nothing was so urgent as keeping Chris out of jail. I'd called Julio and told him what was going on—told him not to come up from Monterey, where he lived. But his daughter was with her mother that weekend and he was lonely, I guess. He didn't care how late I was going to be—he'd come, let himself in, and see me when I got home, he said.

I wasn't happy about that—I was wildly preoccupied—but I was too distracted to say so. I tried not to think of him as Rob and I talked about what to do next. The police might work all weekend—who were we to slack off? But as it happened, we had little choice. Only one of the people whose names we had was home—Vanda Ragusin—and she was just going out. But she could see us first thing in the morning if we'd like.

A capital idea, we thought. We'd call on not only

Vanda, but as many people as we could before noon
the next day—being Saturday, it should be an ideal time
for catching them. And Saturday night, there was a
wake for Jason—a huge one, with everyone at the *Chron*
invited, as well as everybody Jason knew in the music
business and theater. Of course it would be a little odd—
Chris's lawyer showing up, if Chris had been arrested
by then—but I was game.

I went home to find my guest had arrived.

Normally, I would have been thrilled at the sight of
Julio, his elegant body flung casually on my bed,
watching some ancient cowboy movie. But I was exhausted with worry, too tired for polite chitchat.

"Whoa. You look—"

"Don't say it."

"Why not? There's honor in hard labor. You look
like you've been doing some."

"Mind if I step in the shower before I say another
word?"

"Yes." He patted his full lips, lips you could write
a poem about—why, I wondered, wasn't more literary
attention paid to men's lips? "Kiss first," he said,
sounding like Tarzan, looking like a movie star. Or so
I thought, anyway. Julio Soto is one of the handsomest
men on the face of the earth, even if he doesn't like my
car, which is a white Jeep. In which he looks like a
desert prince.

I kissed first, showered second, came out and lay
beside him in a towel, too tired to fossick for clothes.
He wanted to kiss third, but I couldn't even get my lips
to work. "Ten-minute nap?" I pleaded, and he offered
me a lovely nest in the crook of his arm.

It was more like half an hour, I guess, before I stirred,
and Julio said, "You shouldn't wear those high heels,
you know. You get this way when you do."

"Umm. I'll take that under advisement." I was still bleary-eyed.

"Chinese food?"

"God, yes!" I said, not caring a whit that I'd had it for lunch. It meant no decisions—about where to go, what to wear, how to find parking—and that was like a rare gift; it also meant another half hour of lying about.

Finally, though, I made it into a pair of white leggings and a long-sleeved T-shirt, and when Julio came back with the goodies, I ingested with gusto. Feeling human, finally, I brought Julio up-to-date—he knew the outline but not the details. To me, there were mind-boggling matters here—my partner of many years was suspected of murder; she'd been leading a secret life; and she was psychic. Which meant, perhaps, that other intelligent, noncrazy people could be psychic, a possibility I hadn't considered. He was right about the high heels, they did make me tired. But all this new data positively exhausted me. I couldn't remember when I'd been so overwhelmed.

Julio had a slightly different take on the whole thing. "I don't see how you could have been so naive. Why wouldn't there be psychics in the world? Do you think the only things that are real are the ones you can see?"

Did I? I'd never thought about it. "Well," I said slowly. "I'm not exactly an atheist, I just don't think about it much. But that's different anyhow."

"Right. Because it's culturally acceptable, and being psychic isn't."

"How come you accept it, then? You're a scientist."

He shrugged. "I just never thought about not accepting it. Plenty of people say they're psychic and have throughout history. What's the percentage in disbelieving it?"

"You mean, who can be bothered?"

"Right."

Everyone I knew, practically. People with college educations who worked in the professions. No, that would include Julio. A phrase came to me: Urban smartasses. Smug people intolerant of other people's beliefs.

People like me. This was a new way to think of myself. And yet, there were so many crazies in the world, weren't there? People into flower essence therapy, live cell blood analysis, iridology, ayurvedic kinesiology, past life readings, feng shui, shamanic counseling, devic gardening. People like my Cosmic Blind Date. I just lumped them together and assumed everyone else I knew did too. And that was why I was having such a hard time now. I didn't know where Chris really stood in all of this. Had she only pretended she thought Roger DeCampo was crazy? For all I knew she saw ETs herself. Maybe Julio did. I didn't know the answer because we'd never talked about it. It never occurred to most people, I realized, to bring up socially unacceptable beliefs.

"Listen," I said, "where do you stand on ETs?"

"What?" He looked at me as if I'd lost my mind.

"Are they real or not?"

"Who cares?"

"If you met someone who believed in them, would you think they were crazy?"

He thought about it. "Well, I did meet someone like that—girlfriend of a buddy of mine. Said she got kidnapped, the whole bit."

"And was she crazy?"

He shrugged. "Seemed pretty sane, now that I think of it. Why are we talking about this?"

"It's kind of on my mind."

"Well, something's on mine."

"What?"

"Rob Burns. Your old boyfriend."

"You mean my spending time with him?"

"Of course. What do you think I mean? It bothers me."

"You're jealous?"

He considered. "Yeah. I think I'd have to say I am."

I laughed, delighted. "Well, I'm flattered."

"You're not taking this seriously."

"Oh. Well, I guess I don't really understand it yet. It's business—you understand that."

"That doesn't mean I have to like it."

Honestly, I didn't blame him. There was a spark between Rob and me. But on the one hand, it was certainly no threat to Julio. And on the other, I didn't have the least idea how to reassure him.

"I appreciate your telling me," I said. "But I don't know what I can do about it."

He linked his fingers and put his hands behind his head. He was silent, a truly bad sign. Julio had one of the sunniest dispositions I'd ever encountered.

At least he wasn't mad enough to go home. But it might have been better if he had—eventually I had to tell him I had to get some sleep because Rob and I were getting together first thing in the morning. He slept with his back toward me.

CHAPTER 5

Ragusin had invited us for eight-thirty.

What kind of fanatic, I wondered, got up that early on a Saturday? In fact, she wasn't home—probably, I remarked to Rob, jogging an extra mile just because she felt like it. I was glad we had a few minutes—something was bothering me.

"Rob," I said, "I've got to take a more active role in the interviews—I hope you don't mind, but it has to work that way." I'd felt terribly out of control on the one with Adrienne.

"I don't think we can do that. Nobody's going to talk to the lawyer of the main suspect."

"First, nobody knows that's who I am. And second, you know they would. People will talk to anybody."

He grumbled a little, but eventually I won. He didn't have a choice, really—I could walk, and right now, since we both had the names we'd gotten from Adrienne, he needed me more than I needed him.

When Ragusin appeared, it wasn't on foot, it was in a zippy little Alfa, out of which she popped in black jeans and black T-shirt, looking a trifle the worse for wear. We introduced ourselves.

"Let's go have coffee," she said. "Or you can. I'm going to bed pretty soon—I'm a night worker."

She had a cozy cottage in which she could brew a

mean cup of coffee. We sat on wicker furniture while she yawned and talked about herself and Jason.

She wasn't wearing makeup, but even so, I could tell she fit the type he was known to date—very beautiful, very sophisticated. She was probably a little older than Jason, about forty maybe, with a good figure, a little on the thin side, black hair cut in layers, and curious hazel eyes that were almost gold sometimes. Her skin was white and fragile looking. She was probably one of the last people in California who still smoked.

She pulled a cigarette out of her mouth and stared at it. "Sorry about this. I've got a high pressure job. Can't seem to stop."

"What do you do?"

"Disc jockey. All that ad-libbing. Stress city."

"How'd you meet Jason?"

She shrugged. "Some party, I guess. I was the perfect date for him—available for anything before midnight; and then, instant pumpkin."

She sucked at her cigarette as if she were angry.

"Why was that perfect?"

She gave Rob a good hard stare. "Well, I'll tell you because it might be important. But it's definitely not for the paper."

Rob nodded. "We're off the record."

"He didn't, uh . . . he wasn't interested in sex." She was a woman who got right down.

"How long did you date?"

"A couple of months, I guess. He was a great date— attentive, courteous, always took me interesting places. But it never came to more than that—I mean, no Saturday hikes, no Sunday brunches, no hanky, and no panky. It was like he needed me for a front or something—maybe he was gay, I don't know. But there were these good-night kisses, which were getting better and better until we were necking like a couple of teenagers." She stubbed out her cigarette, again taking out her anger on it. "So when I pressed the point, he dumped me."

Neither of us knew what to say.

"Dumped you." I repeated finally.

"He just quit calling. You know how that works." She brushed hair away from her face, obviously trying to keep her dignity.

"Were you mad?"

"You mean, did I kill him? It's pretty hard to work up that much excitement over someone you've never even slept with."

"Well, actually, I didn't mean that. I was just wondering how much you had invested in him at that point."

She nodded before she answered. Rob looked at us as if we were speaking Albanian.

"A lot, I guess. He was so charming and yet he seemed so sad. I'm a sucker for sad."

"I know what you mean. You keep wanting to cheer them up."

She looked at me and smiled. "Ah. A fellow neurotic."

"Did you meet friends of his? Double-date or anything?"

"He knew everyone in town. You couldn't go out with him without running into friends of his."

"But I mean close friends. Intimates."

"Intimates! I doubt Jason McKendrick knew the meaning of the word."

Rob said, "You don't seem that sorry he's dead."

She pulled on a cigarette, no longer angry, thinking things over. "Don't I? I almost cried on the air tonight.

I think it only gets to me when I'm alone. Are you going to the wake?''

We nodded.

"I guess I am too. The point of those things is to make it real—that somebody's really dead.''

When we left, I felt bereft myself and couldn't figure out why. Rob said, ''Creepy, wasn't she?''

I'd kind of liked her. ''Was she?''

"Oh, yeah, like a vampire. Dressed all in black. Anorexic. Killing herself with cigarettes. No wonder he wouldn't have sex with her—it'd be like humping a corpse.''

"And then there's the night job.'' I was beginning to realize she was probably a very depressed woman—what had looked like a failure to grieve was probably just her accustomed lack of affect. Well, that made two—Adrienne was no Little Miss Sunshine herself. And come to think of it, Rob had said she always wore black to the office. I wondered if they were into tattoos and piercing as well. And if that meant S&M. The culture changed so fast it was hard to know what went with what. For all I knew you wore pink polka dots to signify S&M these days.

"Who's next on the list?''

"Let's do another girlfriend. I'm dying to see if we've got a pattern here.''

"How about Felicity Wainwright, the oncologist? What do you bet she's just a bundle of giggles?''

Felicity lived in San Mateo, which meant quite a little drive, so it was midmorning by the time we got there. Our plan to surprise people in their beds was rapidly falling apart.

Her house was lovely—Spanish-style stucco, the house of someone who'd been well rewarded for fighting cancer. I wondered what the job was like. If most patients lived, it was one thing—if they didn't, it must be one of the hardest jobs in the world. She was probably away, I realized; anyone who lived that stressful a life probably beat a retreat on weekends.

But there were two teenagers on her porch, a boy and a girl, the girl eating yogurt and granola, the boy practically doing handstands to amuse her. And it looked as if it was working. She kept putting down her bowl and laughing, sometimes touching brow to knees, holding on to her ankles. She had light red hair that hung to the middle of her back in perfect curls, as if she had an expensive perm, but I was willing to bet she was just lucky. Lucky to have that hair, live in that house, be fourteen and in love. She probably didn't own a single black garment.

"Is this the Wainwright residence?"

"Uh-huh. You want to see my mom?"

I nodded.

"Mo-om!" It was a piercing shriek.

"Yes?"

I'd been expecting a harried parent to rush out the door holding her ears. Instead, a woman rounded the corner of the house, wearing khaki pedal pushers and gardening gloves, which she was pulling off delicately, finger by finger.

"Felicity Wainwright?"

She nodded, wary.

Rob said who he was. "And this is Rebecca Schwartz." No more ID than that, which was fine with me. "I was a friend of Jason McKendrick's. I wonder if you'd mind talking about him with us?"

"For a newspaper story?" She was petite, almost birdlike—and from the look on her face, she'd fly away if the answer was yes.

"Actually . . . not yet. We're very concerned, as you

might imagine. And frankly, we're a little pissed that the police haven't arrested anyone. So, I guess you could say this is background right now—we're trying to find out who had a reason to kill Jason.''

The two kids on the porch were riveted. Wainwright glanced at them nervously. ''Let's go in back, shall we?''

We walked behind her, Rob admiring her tiny, perfect butt. I knew that because I knew him so well, but then anybody would have. Felicity Wainwright was one of those perfectly shaped tiny women who made you feel like picking them up like a baby and counting their fingers and toes. Like her daughter, she was a redhead, copper hair cut short and bouncing about her head in unruly curls. Her face was more pink and white than the usual redhead gold, more a blonde's coloring, and her eyes were a very light blue, azure almost, and they were round, which gave her a look of innocence and youth. She looked almost as much like a teenager as her daughter—and about as likely to wear black. There was something about the curls, or perhaps an Irish-shaped face—elflike, with pointy chin—that made her look merry as the month of May.

She took us to a patio paved with flagstones and seated us at a white table under a Cinzano umbrella. She laid her dirty gardening gloves on the table as if they were white-lace ones and this were a formal occasion. ''Would you like some iced tea?''

''Sure,'' said Rob, though I would have declined, eager to get to the interview. He had told me once that he always accepted beverages, it got people used to the idea that he'd be awhile. So I nodded, going along.

When we were all genteelly sipping, Wainwright said, ''I don't know how I can help, really. I feel like I hardly knew him.''

"We heard you two had been dating."

"Dating. Yes." She frowned. "But not so much lately. God, he was fun. He figured out what my favorite foods were and always made sure he let the chef know in advance—things would just magically appear, variations on themes, you know, different things every time but still all my favorites. And then the chef would come out, and Jason would joke around with him—he just had such an easy manner. But—you know—I hadn't seen him in two weeks, maybe three, when I heard the news. Tell me—there's no question he was murdered, is that right?"

"The police have a couple of witnesses who say he started running to get out of the way, but the car backed up and went for him again."

"My God! Who'd want to do that?"

"We were just wondering if you had any thoughts."

"Not unless it was somebody he skewered in one of those wicked reviews of his. He was a completely hilarious writer, but I was always afraid he'd go too far. Other than that, I wouldn't have any idea because I don't know anything about his life—he was one of those guys who only do small talk." She gave me a wry look, as if to say, You know the type?

"So I take it," said Rob, "that you weren't deeply involved with him."

"You mean was I sleeping with him?"

Rob had the good grace to look taken aback, but she kept talking. "I belong to this group that my friend Trudy calls JerkEnders. We have this little rule—no sex before the tenth date." She laughed. "Only two people have ever managed it, I think, but the theory is you should get to know somebody first. Very obvious, huh? And very nineteenth century. Well, it's this way—either those two people must have dated Jason McKendrick, or maybe he belonged to another branch of it, up in the City.''

''Not exactly Fast Eddie, I take it.''

She spread her hands, not hiding a thing. ''It was kind of refreshing at first. After awhile I got to wondering.''

''Wondering what?''

''What was going on.'' She got Rob in a hammerlock stare. ''It isn't exactly guy behavior.''

''I, uh—I guess not.'' It was all I could do not to laugh out loud. It wasn't every day I got to see Rob Burns get flustered. From the shade of pink he was starting to turn, I gathered his cover had just been blown—that he most assuredly knew guy behavior when he saw it, and he was thinking he'd like to indulge in some with Felicity Wainwright.

I changed the subject, to get him off the spot. ''We hear you're an oncologist.''

She nodded. ''Use lots of sunscreen, and maybe we'll never meet professionally.''

''I was just wondering how you met Jason.''

''At a friend's house—Toby Hunter. I mean at Toby and her husband's house. They had us both to dinner one night.'' She smiled, a little embarrassed, I thought. ''I guess it was a fix-up.''

''Just the four of you?''

''Uh-huh.''

''I guess it was. How did Jason know the Hunters?''

''They have a PR agency—I think with a lot of theatrical clients. I guess it was frustrating because Toby couldn't fix them up with Jason, whom she adored. She was always telling me how funny and urbane he was— all of which was true. I just don't know. . . .''

''What?''

''If there was any there.'' She lifted an eyebrow. ''But

there had to be. A man who takes you out for two months and doesn't make a pass must have *some* kind of explanation for it.''

''Maybe a war wound.''

''Insane wife in the attic.''

''Respects you too much.''

We burst out laughing—somehow, we'd managed to bond. Rob stared, amazed. I said, ''What does Toby think?''

''She thinks a disgruntled actor killed him and just hopes it wasn't one of her clients.''

''I mean about the other thing.''

''Oh. Well, she thinks he's in the closet. What else is there to think? Unless he just doesn't like redheads.''

But of course that couldn't be it because then he wouldn't have asked her out in the first place.

''Do the Hunters know him well?''

''Actually, I don't think so. I think that's the only time they ever had him to dinner. I guess it was dicey, considering their career and his.''

''And how did you know them?''

''I guess . . . that's the sort of thing I'm not supposed to talk about.''

Which told the whole story, of course—that one of them was a patient, Toby, probably. That Toby felt Felicity had saved her life and wanted to pay her back. And so she decided to introduce her to the man of her dreams—and Felicity was a good sport who'd gone along with it.

I liked her. Why, I wondered, wasn't she McKendrick's cup of tea? Why weren't Rob and I each other's?

What was this thing called love?

CHAPTER 6

"So he was gay. I'll be damned—Jason McKendrick."

"Well, it *could* have been a war wound," I said.

"No way. You heard what Felicity said about 'guy behavior.'"

"But Jason must have been complicated—I've been thinking about something."

Rob was driving on the way back to the city to try to catch couple friends and men friends. We'd decided to go for the men first—the better to check out the gay idea.

He looked at me curiously.

"If you work at the *Chron*, you have to make guild scale, right?"

"At least."

"And Jason was a pretty big star and an aggressive guy, so it's reasonable to assume he was paid over scale, right?"

"I got a look at one of his checks once. He was way over scale."

"And are you?"

"Not much—just a little."

"But you live in a pretty nice place. How come Jason lived in a hovel with no furniture?"

"I was wondering about that. And his car was an old wreck."

"Why don't we ask Adrienne what he spent his money on?"

"Good idea. I already did."

"Speedy Gonzalez."

"I phoned to make sure she was okay at her dad's, and just happened to inquire. She doesn't know."

We had three men on our list—Barry Dettman, Cal Perotti, and Bobby Auerbach. Barry was our first stop—we'd been told he was one of Jason's oldest friends, maybe his closest. He lived on Potrero Hill, apparently with another friend. A woman answered the door. Television sounds came from somewhere.

As it turned out, Barry was watching a baseball game he just couldn't miss and agreed to see us only if he could take time out when something important happened. We went for it.

Rob gave him the spiel about who we were, and he nodded, not even looking our way. "Oh, man, oh, man, I could just kill Jason for this—he had a hell of a nerve dying on me." It sounded weird coming from a man I could see only in profile. "Know how we met? Playing softball about a million years ago, in Golden Gate Park. We were both on some bar's team. We had a league, bars that played other bars. I'd just gone to Sanborn-Permenter then." That meant he was an architect. "Oh, man, I loved Jase like a brother."

I said, "It must have upset you the way he didn't take care of himself."

"What?" Now he did look. It was written all over his face: Who is this broad, and what the hell is she talking about?

"I mean his apartment. It was just so depressing."

He stared. "His apartment was depressing?"

"You know, the black walls. No furniture. And the mess—I guess he wouldn't even get a cleaning lady."

His cheeks grew slightly pink. "It's a funny thing. I don't even know if I was ever in it. We used to meet in restaurants, or at the theater sometimes. And of course he came over here—about once a month, I guess. I guess we dropped him off there—a million times maybe—but I never thought about it. In all the years I've known him it just never came up." The announcer said, "There's a play at the plate," and his head turned like a robot's.

"And of course there was that terrible old car."

The side of his face said, "Jason loved that car. Everybody teased him about it." His mouth drew down at the memory.

"Did you know his assistant was living with him?"

"Adrienne. Sure. That was Jason's one bad quality. Boy, he treated that kid bad."

"How do you mean?"

"Well, it's no secret—he had a million women. Clarice and I tried to talk to him, but"—briefly, he turned toward us, then back to the screen—"I guess there's a piece of Jason that just never grew up."

Then, as if he'd had an electric shock, he swiveled to face us. "Omigod. You don't think Adrienne finally . . ."

Rob shrugged. "She says she wasn't his girlfriend. That he was just letting her stay there for a while."

"Oh, no way. The two of 'em tooled around all the time. After she moved in, we started having 'em both over to dinner." His face took on the look of someone reaching back into the past. "They kidded around. They were involved. Believe it."

"Why the other women then?"

His shoulders went up. "Jason was like that—a big kid. Liked to have a pretty woman on his arm, but I guess he was more comfortable with someone like Adrienne. Young, not real smart . . ."

"Malleable."

"Yeah."

"Did he ever get involved with the others, or was all that just for show—so no one would know he was living with his assistant?"

"You bet he got involved. He was crazy about that doctor—Felicity something. You should talk to her."

"We did. She says she hardly knew him."

"Oh, come on. He was nuts about her." He sighed. "Of course, he was nuts about some disc jockey a few months ago, and before that . . . I forget."

"Did you know them?"

"Funny thing was, sometimes we met them—we'd run into Jase at the theater or something—but he never brought them over. He talked about them, though. He and I'd go out and shoot a few baskets, something like that, he always had some new lady friend."

"But he always dumped them."

"I don't know. He didn't keep them long; that's all I know."

I said, "What we were wondering was, did any of them go off the deep end when he dumped her? Did he ever talk about one of them acting strange?"

"Well, one used to call him a lot at work. But Adrienne mentioned that, not him. I know what you're getting at, but if he had any enemies, I don't know about them. I still can't believe somebody murdered him. Those witnesses were probably wrong, you know what I mean? You know how people can think they saw something they didn't?" Suddenly a tear popped out of his eye, and he turned quickly away, not wiping it, which would have drawn attention to it.

Neither of the other men friends were home, so we took a desperately needed lunch break and called on a couple, Nick and Susie Rodenborn. They had known him as long as anyone, Adrienne had said, Nick having been his mentor years ago when he'd first come to the *Chronicle*. Rob could remember him—a white-haired editor who'd left to teach college journalism; a kindly sort who had taken the raw material of a brash young man with a brand-new diploma and a ton of ambition and made him the extraordinary writer Jason had been when he died.

Despite the hair, he didn't look old—probably about fifty or thereabouts, but he had an avuncular presence, and I could see why Adrienne had put the Rodenborns on the list of "couple" friends and Barry (though obviously part of a couple) on the men's list. Barry was a basket-shooting kind of pal and clearly these were parent figures. Susie was also white-haired, and plump, very pretty, I thought, but not someone whose appearance mattered a great deal to her. And from what I was learning of Jason, perhaps the only kind of woman he could relate to as a friend.

"Bullshit!" said Rob later. "You heard Barry. He and Adrienne were friends, if nothing else."

"All he said was they kidded around—not that he confided in her."

"Well, guys don't do that much."

"Tell me about it."

The Rodenborns seated us in their living room, a place of smart sofas and halogen lamps, the most conventional room we'd seen that day. But Susie was an artist, and there were odd pictures on the walls—of cats bringing gifts, not of mice, but of swimming pools, espresso makers, burglar alarms, even a Barbie doll. They were very funny, and I was entranced.

"Susie's pussy period," said Nick. "Last year she did dragons."

I must have looked puzzled.

"Of course, they were all wearing darling designer outfits, fully accessorized."

I thought I could like Susie. A lot. She had blue eyes and a warm, round face. I wished that sometime, somehow, I could achieve the self-confidence to look the way she did, but it just isn't in the genes. My mom has standing appointments with so many waxers, cutters, filers, and peelers I don't know how she works in shopping for her state-of-the-art wardrobe. She despairs of her two politically correct daughters (not that she isn't p.c. as well, just a very well-groomed feminist), but, still, I'd like to see the day I let my hair go gray.

Susie turned to me. "We miss Jason so, so much—already. Did you know him well, my dear?"

"I didn't, really. Rob was his friend."

"Oh? Are you new at the *Chronicle*?

It was the first time I'd been challenged. I took a deep breath—I wasn't after anything I could use in court, but you never knew, and lying's never a good idea. I said, "I have another interest in this, to tell you the truth. The police are investigating my law partner in connection with Jason's death." I liked Susie a lot, and Nick seemed like a fine man whom Rob knew—these people were known quantities, I told myself. And took a chance. "They found her name in Jason's pocket, but she didn't know him. Rob is a friend of hers, too, so one of the things we're trying to find out is why it was there."

Nick, true to the professorial image, pulled a pipe from his pocket and began fiddling with it. "If she's an attractive young woman, that could go a long way toward explaining it."

I said, "He seemed to like a lot of very different types of women."

"Oh?" said Nick. "They seemed all of a piece to

me. Beautiful, intelligent, successful—thoroughly acceptable in every way.''

''Acceptable seems a funny word to use. I mean, wouldn't 'desirable' be more to the point?''

Nick said to Rob: ''Quick study, this lady.'' Rob looked confused, and Nick turned back to me. ''You got it, all right. He had women, but there was something passionless about it—like they were just so many appendages to his image.''

''So you think he was an image-oriented man.''

''Either that,'' said Susie, ''or he had something to hide—if only from himself.''

''You thought he was gay?''

''I've wondered. I can't say I haven't wondered. It's funny—when he came to dinner here, he never brought anyone.''

''Not even Adrienne?''

''Adrienne? Who on earth is that?''

Rob said, ''His assistant. About twenty-two, looks like a punk rocker.''

Nick exhaled a cloud of pungent smoke. ''Come on! He wouldn't be caught dead with someone like that.''

''Well, she might have been the thing he had to hide. She was living with him, but she says they were just roomies. On the other hand, his friend Barry Dettman swears they were lovers.''

''We never even heard of her!'' Susie sounded put out.

I said, ''Jason was a man with secrets.''

Nick took a few puffs. ''When we first met he didn't even want to say where he was from. Then later, I met his sister, who'd moved here from wherever it was—I'm still not sure—and found out coincidentally that that's who she was. Jason had never even mentioned her.''

''But here's the question,'' I said, ''was he just a

secretive kind of guy? Or did he really have something to hide?''

"I got inklings of that," said Nick. "That's why I brought all this up. But they were only that. You know, some people really are just that way. It's their nature."

"Darling," said Susie, "do you think we ought to tell them . . ." She stopped there, waiting for him to make the connection.

"About Tommy?" he said, and she nodded.

"You two know who Tommy La Barre is?"

"The guy who owns Dante's?"

The Rodenborns nodded.

Rob whistled. "That's big medicine."

It was. Dante's was a well-known, fairly new, extremely popular San Francisco restaurant. Like some of the City's oldest restaurants, it had private dining rooms upstairs. However, it had turned out that more than dining was happening there. A high-stakes poker game—very high stakes—occurred every Friday night. That was one thing. The other was the young ladies. Like the poker game, they were available only to certain clientele—but they were most certainly available. Or so the D.A. claimed. But the case was still pending, and somehow, Tommy was keeping his restaurant open.

There had been so much publicity that whatever Tommy's original story, if he hadn't by now become a pimp and gambling host, he was missing a great opportunity—anyone with money who wanted some action now knew where to go.

"How does he fit in?" I asked.

"He was a friend of Jason's," said Susie. "A close friend. Jason was fascinated with him, but then who wouldn't be? I admit I am myself. We even begged Jase to let us take him to dinner at Dante's, so we could meet him, but somehow he never got around to it."

She stopped and sighed. "When I'm done with the cats, I think I might do gentlemen thugs. What do you think?"

But Rob and I were too riveted to answer.

In the car he said, "You know, he's got to be mob. Where there's gambling and whores, there's mob."

"And usually drugs. And where there's drugs, there's murder."

"He might not be mob. It's such a small operation over there—maybe he's just a weird dude with a yen to please his rich friends."

"And make a few bucks on the side. The exclusivity of the thing argues for that. Anyway, let's put mob aside for a minute and just say Tommy thickens the plot pretty irresistibly. Jason had some kind of weird sex thing going, right?"

"Not necessarily—he might have been gay. Or involved with Adrienne."

"Okay, let me rephrase. He was probably hiding something about sex."

"Granted."

"Well, La Barre was perfect. He could get Jason whatever he wanted—discreetly."

"Like what?"

"I don't know—ladies who'd beat him or ladies who'd wear a dog collar and walk on a leash. Ladies who'd talk dirty or watch him beat off or let him watch them—whatever he was into."

"It certainly opens up a world of possibilities, but still. What was the motive? And here's a tougher one. How would a guy like Tommy La Barre know Chris?"

"I thought you'd never ask."

The response was gratifying, but he nearly wrecked the car. What happened was, he turned to stare and forgot to watch the road. After we nearly got creamed by a taxi, and I nearly blew his eardrums out with a terrified screech, and he'd straightened the car out, and said, "don't do that to me," I told him what I knew.

"He came to see Chris a few months ago—"

"To get her to take the case!"

"No. A little twist on it—to get her to do his divorce. A well-known feminist lawyer would be ideal, wouldn't she? For something like that. For a guy with his reputation. Anyway, she slept on it, and that was what she decided he must be thinking, and she felt used. Also, she realized he made her feel like she was covered with motor oil."

"So she turned him down."

"Yes, and he yelled at her and insulted her. I guess it's the sort of thing you pretty much forget the next day—she was just glad to have him out of her life—but if he was a pretty sick guy . . ."

"Oh, man. This could be it."

CHAPTER 7

Chris was sure it was. Before Rob took me home, we dropped by her house and made her day. She covered her right eye with one hand, in the careless and, to me, supremely Southern gesture she made when she was overcome with amazement.

"Oh my God. He said things like, 'You can't do this to me. Nobody shines Tommy La Barre on.' Then he sort of did this slow, disgusted glance around and said, 'Look at your office. You can't afford to turn me down. This could have made your pathetic little career.' "

"And I suppose he left, saying, 'You'll regret the day . . .' or something like that."

"You know something? He did. The guy was slug spit, I'm telling you. And I don't see how Jason McKendrick could have been a decent person either, if he was friends with him."

But I did. I had to agree with Susie Rodenborn on that one. A man like that was fascinating. The dangerous, the shady, the criminal, the other—even the evil—had a malign appeal; if kept at a distance, of course. Maybe Jason had gotten too close.

I thought about that awhile—the other. And wondered why Roger DeCampo hadn't been more fascinating. The answer was simple, I thought—because we were operating in two separate realities. You couldn't make a connection with someone like that. Evil—if that's what La Barre was—was part of all of us, something all too familiar that we never, never for any reason acknowledged in ourselves. And so we gave it so someone else—Jeffrey Dahmer, Richard Nixon, whoever was in the neighborhood. You didn't want to make a connection with it—you just wanted to reassure yourself it was out there instead of in here, and so you liked to get it where you could watch it. I've always been suspicious of people who get squeamish when you bring up violent crime—they don't even want to think it's out there, which is even scarier. With no evil in the world, surely they couldn't do any. Such people must have unhappy spouses and children.

"Uh, Rebecca," said Rob. "Are you with us?"

I'd been staring into space, quietly giving myself the willies.

He said, "We have to get going."

"I want to talk to Chris," I said, and turned to her. "Could you take me home in a bit?"

"Sure. I need the company anyway—you two get to go out, but I don't." She meant to the wake. Under the circumstances, we'd thought, it was best if she didn't go.

Rob said, "Pick you up at eight?"

When he'd gone, Chris said, "What's wrong? You still mad at me?"

"I'd say you were psychic, but you're only half right. I wasn't mad until I started thinking it over."

"And now?"

"Well, I'm not sure I know who you are anymore. I mean, every time you make fun of Shirley MacLaine, you're a hypocrite."

"I've never in my life made fun of Shirley Mac-Laine."

"You haven't? Yes, you have—I've heard you do it."

"Uh-uh. You've seen me trying to titter politely when everyone else is doing it. Matter of fact"—she kicked at her coffee table with a sock-clad foot—"I hate it when people do that. There's this kind of socially acceptable list of beliefs if you're college educated and live on one of the coasts. I was at a dinner party the other night where someone said, 'My ex-boyfriend just converted to Christianity, isn't that disgusting?' And nobody said a word. A couple of people just said, 'Ohmigod,' like it was the worst thing they could think of."

"I don't get it. You're not a Christian. Are you?" Who knew what she was anymore.

"No, Rebecca, I am not a Christian. I have never been and I will never be a Christian, though I come from a family of devout Presbyterians. I can't imagine having the least interest in a religion that denigrates both sex and women like Christianity does. But I am still an American, and I'm absolutely shocked at the way people go around attacking each other's religions. If my ex-boyfriend converted to Christianity, I might think it's disgusting, too, but I most assuredly wouldn't feel free to say so in public. I think it's a lot more disgusting that people think it's perfectly okay to do that. Unless we're talking Judaism or Zen, of course— if you attacked a Jew or a Zennie, you'd be anti-Semitic or narrow-minded, depending. Definitely not okay to attack the sacred cows. Those two are fine—and Catholicism because Catholics are pretty vocal and they're a minority in a way. Episcopalianism because it's so perfectly starched and therefore perceived as hardly a religion at all. Mennonites and Quakers are off the hook because they're exotic; Unitarians because they're so intellectual . . . and that's about it. Forget it if you're a Moslem or a Lutheran.''

But I was barely listening. My heart was going like a car engine. My throat was closing. Was Chris anti-Semitic? I thought back to what she'd said: Judaism was a sacred cow. Wasn't that an anti-Semitic remark? It couldn't be, because Chris had said it—the same way psychics must exist because she was one. I had to think this over; I had to digest it. And right now I wanted answers about what I'd already thought over.

''You're as bad as anybody else. You said Roger DeCampo was crazy when all he did was say he had friends who'd seen ETs. And you go around hearing voices!''

''I do not hear voices—that's clairaudient, and I'm a classic clairvoyant. Roger Whizbang is clearly crazy because he's obsessed—not because he thinks aliens exist.''

''But you don't know that. For all you know he had an experience like me—he went around all his life thinking there probably weren't ETs, the same way I thought psychics were frauds—and then his best friend tells him he's been kidnapped by little green men. What's he supposed to do with that? I mean if a sane and rational person told him—''

''Ohmigod!'' She put her hand over her eye in that way she has. ''You're right. I *am* as bad as anybody else. I really am.'' She sat quietly for a minute, and then she said, ''Thank you for pointing that out.''

''That's okay,'' I said. ''I guess I am too.''

''No. You stood up for the guy—I mean, you didn't fall in love with him, but you didn't condemn him as a maniac. And I guess I did.''

''It isn't that—it's that I haven't even read Shirley

MacLaine. And I've probably spent *hours* making fun of her.''

So we cleared the air a little—though I still had food for thought—and ended up with a great big sloppy hug. But I still went home feeling empty and isolated. It was nothing to do with Chris's diatribe on religious intolerance—and the more I thought about it, I thought maybe she had a point—but everything to do with the loneliness I felt at learning I didn't really know her.

And it was only exacerbated by the way Rob and I had spent the day—pursuing Jason McKendrick's secret. It was abundantly obvious he had at least one . . . more than one. Adrienne was a secret from the Rodenborns, and the fact that she was only his roommate was a secret from Barry Dettman—or else she *was* his lover and that was a secret from us.

Did everyone have secrets? Did Rob? Did Julio?

Did I?

I thought about it. What were secrets about in our society? Sex, usually. We Americans were still as puritanical as the Pilgrims. If not sex, then what? Crime. That was a big one. Embezzling. Insider trading. Cheating on your income tax. Then there was money. Especially if crime was involved. What else? I had to admit Chris was right. Religion. ''Weird'' beliefs, meaning any that were different from—well she *was* right—from the sacred cows. If you wanted to practice law in this town, you'd better not be psychic. If you wanted to be considered intelligent and taken seriously, you probably shouldn't get born again. But something nagged at me here—Chris was right about sex and women, too—Christianity did denigrate them. So how *could* an intelligent person be a Christian? I heard a little voice—did this mean I was psychic?—saying: *How's Judaism on those issues?*

No better, came the answer. And yet you *could* be intelligent if you were Jewish. What if you were something really outside the norm? Better keep it a secret.

Other secrets I thought of: Addictions. Eating disorders. Health problems. These were the things you didn't talk about—unless, in the case of the former two, you were in "recovery." I realized that I had mentally put quotes around the word—denigrating someone else's way of talking about his belief system, his life. Chris was *so* right—mocking was second nature. And the realization of it made me feel horribly isolated.

Feeling grumpy and weird (was "weird" a judgmental, isolating word?), I stepped in the shower. Water is a great calmer.

And yet, by the time I stepped out, I was more upset. Near panicked, in fact. Because in the course of my shower, I found a lump in my breast.

I pushed the panic down. It couldn't be there. I had felt a rib, that must be it. But I was too ragged to make sure right now—I'd do it in the morning. I made that a promise to myself: I'd check it first thing in the morning.

Okay then, I had to get ready to go say good-bye to Jason McKendrick, someone I'd never even known. I wished I had time to play the piano—I knew that would lift me out of the doldrums. But I didn't. I put some baroque music on the stereo and applied myself to the task of picking out something to wear. I had a new dress that would probably be perfect—ankle-length black crepe. But somehow I'd been meaning to wear it to something more cheerful. If I put it on now it would always make me sad—it would remind me of the day I knew I was going to have a mastectomy, that I was probably going to die. . . . The music obviously wasn't working. Suddenly, I just wanted to get out of the house.

I slipped on a pair of black pants, a gray silk blouse, and a tapestry vest. I hoped the effect was sober enough. My mood certainly was.

I waited downstairs for Rob, something I've probably never done before, and found the air felt good, the velvet of the night did a lot to still the panic.

Rob was five minutes early. "Am I late?"

"Not at all. I was just restless." He gave me a funny look, and on the short drive I was aware of his trying to start conversations and of my trying to participate, but I was so unfocused nothing ever really went anywhere.

It was the only wake I've ever been to where there was valet parking. It was being held in a sort of dance hall whose proprietors had been friends of Jason's. The whole idea, it seemed, was for every entertainer who'd ever known Jason to play a song or give a speech in his memory. A no-host bar was doing a good business, and people were milling, talking, only half listening to the earnest performers. It was an eerie scene, frankly. Because of the performances, the place was dark, yet it had the curious quality of a gathering where people had gone to be seen. Some people, anyhow—I saw the mayor there, and a couple of assemblymen.

Everyone I knew from the *Chronicle* was there—and there were plenty; when Rob and I were dating, we'd been to lots of *Chronicle* parties together. And there were other people I recognized, from the society and entertainment pages, from television news. Genuine grief hung in the air along with scent of celebrity. Jason had been a popular man—this shindig was invitational, though signs had been posted at the *Chron* and backstage at certain theaters. I found myself wishing I'd known him—a person so complicated he could live in filth and poverty and never, I gathered, invite anyone to his apartment, yet be so influential, so well liked that the city's celestial beings turned out at his death.

Rob went off to work the room, leaving me to do the same if I chose, and I did. It was the surest way of forgetting my own troubles and a golden opportunity as well. I went to get a glass of wine and found myself standing in line behind a man in a suit and a tie with a stain on it, a middle-aged man with a red, sad face and a voice that carried. He had buttonholed the woman in front of him, a stranger from the look on her face.

"Would you look at that?" He pointed to the stain on his tie. "Some asshole just bumped into me, never even said excuse me. Whole drink splattered all over."

The woman shook her head as if to say that was a shame, but she didn't really want to talk to him.

"Place is full of assholes, you notice that? Nothin' but assholes, the whole damn place."

The woman's smile froze, and she turned around. That made the drunk mad. "Hey! You an asshole, too? Huh? What's your problem? You too good to talk to a hick from across the Bay?"

I wondered if there was a bouncer. He was getting so loud it was time for somebody to do something. Suddenly I was aware of motion behind me, and a black blur came up on my left.

"Dad! Dad, you've gotta calm down."

It was Adrienne. She recognized me and looked embarrassed, but she couldn't be bothered with that now. She was stage-whispering to her dad: "You just don't know how loud your voice is. They're going to throw us out of here if you don't quiet down."

"Goddammit, I don't care if they do! I didn't want to come to this goddam thing in the first place."

"Okay." She stopped whispering, the urgency gone. Her voice was low and placating. "Okay, Dad, you're

right. Let's just leave. I'll take you home right now.
Come on now. Let's just go.''

"I want a drink." His voice was low also, for the
first time, and sulky.

"I don't know, I don't think . . ." But the bartender
by this time was asking him what he wanted. Adrienne
shrugged and turned to me. "Hi."

"Hi. You doing okay?" It couldn't be restful, being
holed up in El Cerrito with this character.

"Yeah." She inclined her head toward her father.
"Dad's fine except when he drinks. It's good being with
him. I cook for him, and I forget Jason for a little while.
Things were going so well I forgot what happens—you
know." She glanced at him again. "I shouldn't have
asked him to come tonight. He's introspective, you
know what I mean? Not much of a social animal."

Downright misanthropic, I would have said, but it
wouldn't have been polite. Besides it was my turn at
the bar, and Adrienne had her hands full with her dad,
trying to lead him to a corner where there weren't so
many assholes.

I saw Rob talking to a dark-haired woman, very thin,
in a black dress that showed her fashionable bod for
what it was—a grape stake. She had shoulder-length hair
parted on the side and falling in such perfect waves that
jealousy was the only sane response. She wore gold
hoop earrings and a slash of lipstick—if she had on
more makeup than that, it was so skillfully applied no
one was the wiser. There was nothing flashy about this
woman, no ruby lips, azure eyes, the sort of thing poets
go on about. Just a quiet perfection. But for some reason Rob looked desperate to get away from her.

I walked over, thinking to rescue him. "Rebecca,
this is Jason's sister, Tressa Gornick."

I said I was sorry for her loss, or words to that effect.

"It's funny," Rob said, "I was just telling Tressa that Jason never talked about his family much. I don't think many of us knew he even had a sister."

"I'm from back East," she said woodenly, her eye scanning the room.

"Oh? Where?"

She shrugged. Her voice was like ice. "I don't really feel much like talking about that."

I understood Rob's discomfort—the woman was clearly snubbing him, and was now snubbing me as well—yet there was a problem extricating oneself. "Nice talking to you," in the face of obvious rudeness seemed like a putdown. But what else to do?

Rob—ever the intrepid reporter—tried another gambit: "And your parents?"

"Dead." She didn't look at either of us. Her tone was robotic.

"Ah. Well. I'm sorry."

And miraculously we were saved. Her eyes lit up at the sight of a tall man approaching with a drink. "There you are," she said, and we beat a hasty retreat.

I said, "In shock, do you think?"

"Who, me? Definitely."

"Morticia." I wagged my chin at Jason's sister.

"Could be. Must be. Why come if you're just going to insult your relative's friends?"

Guilt, I supposed. Family obligation. A promise perhaps. Plenty of reasons besides familial love. But it certainly seemed as if Tressa Gornick was mad at someone; I wondered if it was her brother.

"Holy shit! There's somebody I haven't seen in years."

He was off again. I listened again to the band onstage, quite enjoying myself, but focus is a fragile thing and anyway there was lots to look at—faces, fashion statements, vignettes. My eye caught a woman leaning against a pillar, her hands behind her back, alone.

So totally alone: this was what her pose said. It drew attention to itself by its very melodrama.

Intrigued, I moved closer and thought I heard a whimper. Not wanting to intrude on her privacy, but curious, let's face it, I stole another glance. Tears were wearing ruts in her makeup; her jaw was trembling as she struggled for control. She must have felt me looking at her, for her head turned and she caught me. She looked so miserable that I forgot my embarrassment; my heart went out to her, and I rummaged without thinking in my purse. Coming up with a tissue, I held it out.

"Thanks," she said, and I know she meant to smile, but a grimace was all she managed.

"You must have known him well," I said.

She nodded. "We were lovers."

I was taken aback, both by the starkness of the statement—an extraordinary thing to say to a perfect stranger—and by its source. This woman was no Felicity Wainwright and no Vanda Ragusin. These two were wildly different, but their similarities were so obvious they'd been mentioned by everyone who knew Jason: he went out with gorgeous, bright, with-it ladies. He was famous for it.

This girl was younger and less sure of herself, but nothing like as young and vibrant as Adrienne. In fact, if I had to say what she was missing, vibrancy would be the easiest word to use. She had lackluster skin, freckled and poorly cared for. Her hair hung unfashionably to her chin, which was too broad for that length—and for the current ideal of female beauty. Her face was simply unremarkable—a pleasant enough face, and probably more so when it wasn't swollen from crying, but she wasn't blessed with burning eyes or flying cheekbones; it was just a face. Her body was lumpy—she wasn't much overweight, perhaps twenty pounds or so, but her posture was poor and she looked soft, as if she didn't exercise, had too little self-esteem even to bother. Her clothes were frankly frumpy—she wore a denim skirt and cotton turtleneck, two items she'd obviously just happened to find somewhere in her closet, and, on the spur of the moment, deemed suitable to wear together. The skirt was straight, a mini, and at least a size too small. She wore black tights beneath it.

And this was the woman who—cast doggedly against type—had apparently captured Jason's heart. Or maybe she was lying. She was so tentative, so unsure of herself I couldn't imagine her with Jason—with the demanding person I thought he was. "I'm so sorry," I said. "Had you been together long?"

She shook her head. "Oh. No. It was awhile back."

"It's still hard," I said. "I'm Rebecca Schwartz, by the way."

"I'm Sarah Byers."

"Have you seen Tressa—his sister?"

"Oh! I didn't know he had one." So she hadn't known him all that well.

"How did you and Jason meet?"

"I was sitting on a bar stool one night and he sat right down next to me. We both knew the bartender so"—she smiled shyly—"so you could say we were properly introduced."

"Rebecca!" It was Rob. I felt my elbow grabbed and guided away. "Could I borrow you a minute?" As I pivoted and joined him—it was either that or fall down—I heard him say to Sarah, "Could you excuse us, please?"

"Bye, Sarah," I called over my shoulder. "I hope I see you again."

"Guess who's here?" said Rob.

"The governor, maybe? Must be somebody really important, to merit that performance."

"It's Tommy La Barre."

Tommy had been called onstage, and he was climbing up now. In a few minutes he was weeping, getting himself all worked up with funny anecdotes about his good buddy, Jason. I looked over at Sarah's pillar, but she was gone.

CHAPTER
8

The lump was still there the next morning. Already, it was The Thing, the size of a mountain and about as insurmountable. I *had* to forget about it—it was the only survival.

I wished, wished, wished I had Julio with me—maybe I could drive to Monterey and see him.

I dialed but got no answer. Not a good sign for first thing in the imorning.

Nothing was stopping me from hopping in the car, but I couldn't bear it if I did and got more bad news. Technically (according to our agreement) we were perfectly free to date other people, but I certainly hoped he wouldn't. I was rather flattered that he didn't even like my working with Rob, but what if he used that as an excuse to find a babe?

I was nuts today, I decided. All the more reason not to pop down to Monterey. Normally Chris could have been a tower of strength, but she needed to lean on me right now—I certainly couldn't tell her what was going on.

But won't she know anyway? I wondered. *What if I met her for brunch and she came up to the table and said, Omigod! your whole chest is black. What's wrong with you, Peachblossom?*

I didn't know how this psychic thing worked yet—if I was dying I wanted to hear it from a doctor.

That left my sister, Mickey. Which would have been wonderful except that she was half of a couple and the other half was someone I wanted to see like a troop of IRS goons. But Mickey it had to be.

My luck: Kruzick answered the phone. "Kittens 'R Us. Mehitabel speaking."

" '*Toujours gai* and always a lady, that's my motto, Archy.' "

"Watch who you're calling gay. You want the black one or the calico?"

"Omigod! Lulu!" I'd forgotten their cat was pregnant.

"Mother and cuties resting comfortably. All seven of them."

"*In the midst of death* . . ." I thought, and all of a sudden I had to see those kittens. "I'll be right over."

I couldn't take one, of course—I had fish, a hundred-gallon saltwater aquarium in my living room. But I could pick them up and feel their furry newness, their heartbreaking innocence; hear their pathetic little mews; and wish all of life was baby animals. Why, I thought, not for the first time, had we screwed up our lives with machines? I'd gladly give up television and computers for a life of calves and kittens and goslings. Or so I thought sometimes—when I chose to ignore my deep gratitude for indoor plumbing and antibiotics, the two greatest inventions of modern times.

Mickey and Alan were on their way out to a brunch, which left once again a deep hole in my day. I must have looked as miserable as I felt because Mickey asked me to dinner the next night, and Alan said, "Don't bother coming in till Thursday—I've cancelled everything."

"What?" I was suddenly panicked. "I appreciate

your enthusiasm for the cause, but I've got to make a living.''

"You didn't have anything that couldn't wait. You were just going to look at your calendar and tell me to do it anyway.''

Actually, he was right. What I mostly needed to do was spend a lot of time preparing a case that was set for trial in a month, so I'd already pared down my schedule. I sighed—it was as good a time as any for Chris to get in trouble.

I went home and called Rob. No answer.

Julio again. No answer.

Halfheartedly, I looked up Sarah Byers in the phone book. She was definitely someone I had to speak to, but maybe not today. Yet I really should, I felt. She was in the book—at least there was an S. Byers, whom I promptly dialed. A machine answered: "Hi, this is Sarah. . . .''

Okay, fine. She lived on Green Street near Polk, more or less Russian Hill; very Chinese the last few years. I popped over and rang her bell.

Even Sarah Byers wasn't home that fine Sunday when I needed someone to talk to.

I sat in my car, thinking. I could always go to a movie. That was a good escape. Or play the piano—but the mood I was in, I'd just play dark, draggy dirges and make things worse. What I needed was open spaces, contact with nature, more kittens.

I could go hiking by myself, but I didn't think that was smart.

I could drive to Marin County—but since I'd grown up there, it was too familiar to afford an escape and besides, my parents lived there. Once across the bridge, I'd probably drive obsessively to their house, and that was the last thing I needed.

I wanted support, but I didn't want to be reduced to a child, and I've found, like most people I know that it takes extreme lightness of foot to maintain adult status in the presence of one's parents. I wasn't up to it today.

Having perfectly rationalized my decision, under the illusion that I'd exhausted all my options, I then turned my car south and headed where I wanted to go in the first place—to Monterey. If Julio still wasn't home, the worst that could happen was I'd have a great little drive and a beautiful walk on the beach. There was nothing like sea air for spiritual renewal—that and your lover's arms.

Well, he wasn't home. It was mid-afternoon by then—about three o'clock—and I was starving. So I went to the wharf and had a crab sandwich. Then that walk on the beach, which truly was invigorating, renewing, and thoroughly salutary. But lonesome. Marriage, I thought, would be good for times like this.

The buddy system probably wasn't a bad way to get through life. Now that my career was established, I really ought to give some thought to it. Suddenly I wondered: Why the hell aren't I married, anyway? I'm such a *good* girl.

It was unlike me to overlook an important matter of conformity; I have a very chicken-hearted streak under my tough lawyer's exterior. I'd certainly done everything else the culture said I should do—it must be, I realized, that I hadn't felt particularly pressured to get married. Perhaps women had made some progress after all. I was cheered by the thought, but only a little—I figured I was probably wrong.

There still being no Julio, I did what I could as easily have done in San Francisco—went to a movie. And afterward, there was a light in Julio's house. My heart lurched—I hadn't realized how eager I was to see him (though hanging around all day should have been a clue).

But a strange voice answered the door—a young, female one. "Who is it?"

"Rebecca. Is Julio home?"

Instantly, the door swung open and a tiny gold-colored girl launched herself at me. I just had time to brace or I'd have been knocked over completely. "Esperanza! Baby, baby, how are you?"

She didn't answer, just kept her face buried somewhere around my midriff. A teenage girl hovered uncertainly in the background—the baby-sitter, I realized.

When I'd come loose from Esperanza, been pulled into the house, I told the baby-sitter my name and learned hers was Tiffany.

"She's our friend, Tiffany. She'll take over," said Esperanza. "You can go home now."

But Tiffany and I knew it wasn't quite that simple. "Tell you what," I said. "I'll stay a little while, and Tiffany can have a break and watch TV—then I've really got to get back home."

"No." She fashioned her exquisite lips into a pout.

"Why not?"

"Stay all night."

"Honey, tomorrow's a school day for me." *And anyway, your dad doesn't need two dates in one evening.* It was killing me not to ask where he was.

"I just got back from Mom's, and Dad went out!"

"Well, sweetheart, I'm here." I tried to keep my mind off Julio, talking brightly and fast. I asked civilized questions about our pals Libby and Keil, and what Esperanza was doing in school, until eventually I noticed my stomach was rumbling.

Esperanza had eaten, so I asked if I could make my-

self something, but she came right back at me: "I'll
make you some eggs."

"You can make eggs? Who taught you?" I was instantly sorry I'd asked the question.

But she only said, "I took a cooking class. Daddy'll
be back soon." She looked wistful, as if she were afraid
I'd leave if I didn't think that.

"Honey, that's okay. I'm happy just being here with
you."

She smiled and sat down to tell me all about sixth
grade, which, so far as I could gather, was mostly about
which recording artists were the best: "So then in the
video there's these two Valley girls and one of them
says, 'Would you *look* at her butt! It is so biiig. . . .'
You know how they make every word separate, like
each one is some sort of *event*?"

I was howling. She did a very funny Valley girl. But
she stopped in the middle. "So, how're *you*? I mean,
is everything all right?"

"Why, do I look sick?"

"You never, like, just show up. Dad always tells me
if you're coming. Anyhow, he couldn't have known or
he'd be here. So something must be wrong."

"No, I just . . ." Was I going to lie? What was the
point? "I just felt a little lonesome, that's all."

Tiffany came in. "Bedtime."

"She's right, honey. We're being bad."

"Are you leaving?" She badly wanted me to stay;
why, I wasn't sure—to reassure herself, probably, that
things were okay between Julio and me.

"I have to get up early. But I'll be down soon. Next
weekend, maybe." If I were invited.

She held on to me a long time and looked terribly
sad when I left. She missed her own mother, I knew;
and when she was with Silvia, Julio's ex-wife, she

missed her dad; and me, I thought. She missed me, too.

I was looking forward to the drive back, feeling the bittersweetness of Esperanza's good night, the outright sadness of not having seen Julio, but resigned, ready for an hour and a half of singing along with the radio. However, as I was waving good-bye, I heard a voice say, "What on earth is a Jeep doing in my driveway?"

So I agreed to stay awhile, and Esperanza went to bed happy. Tiffany, it developed, lived across the street and didn't have to be taken home. In seconds, Julio and I were alone. He'd been on a date, I was pretty sure— his sheepish look more or less confirmed it. But it couldn't have been much of one because he was home early. And anyway, we had the damn agreement.

The reason we had it was that we both recognized neither one of us could leave the place where we lived— I practiced law in the city, which was like lifeblood to me anyhow; and Julio was a marine biologist at the Monterey Bay Aquarium. How much future did such a relationship have? So he had a right to date and I had a right to date because we were both adults and we recognized these things.

Ftah.

That was the way I felt, but I kept my mouth shut.

He got me some wine and said the same stuff Esperanza had said: Was I all right? Why was I there?

"I just wanted to see you. I guess I'm depressed."

"About Chris?"

It would have been a perfect time to say: No! I'm depressed because this time next week I'll have no breasts and this time next year I'll be dead. Or similar calm words.

Instead, I said, "I guess so." Which was partly true. "I mean, not about her being investigated—I can deal with that. About having to reassess my relationship with her.''

"You know what? I get the feeling it's not that simple."

"That's not complicated enough?"

"I've been thinking about our conversation Friday. I realize a lot of your beliefs are being called into question."

"*My* beliefs? Wait a minute, Chris is—"

He held up a hand. "Hold it, hold it. Let me explain. You think everything can be explained in rational terms, right?"

I was puzzled. "Of course."

"And this thing of Chris's—I mean, having the nerve to be psychic when everybody knows there's no such thing—it just can't be explained that way. So to believe it, you have to uproot everything you ever thought."

"No, I don't. Psychic could be scientific. I mean, what if our brains emit waves, like radio waves . . .''

"Sure, sure, sure. It could be science, but science doesn't recognize it. And nothing in this culture's worth a dime if science doesn't recognize it."

"Well, you're a scientist. What's wrong with that?"

"What's wrong with that is it's bullshit."

The room spun around me, exactly as if I was about to lose consciousness. If Chris's defection from the world of reason had been a blow, what was this?

Et tu, Julio? Tell me I'm not alone out here.

He said, "Have you ever met someone and disliked him or her on sight? Even down to a prickling at the back of your neck?"

"You think that's psychic?"

"I think you're taking in information in a nonrational way. Call it vibes or energy. . . .''

I mimed gagging.

"Oh, don't be so closed-minded." Which was more or less what Chris had said. "What's so great about the intellect, anyway?"

"What?" Had he gone mad? Had the world?

"I mean, what's it done for us? It hasn't kept us from making a hole in the ozone; turning the air to poison; destroying the rain forests."

I might have said something about antibiotics and plumbing, but I was too astonished.

I said, "What would you put above the intellect?"

"Nothing. But there are sure as hell some things I'd give equal weight to. The heart, for instance—how we feel."

That part made me go weak in the knees—Rob Burns would never have said a thing like that.

"And the body. In a lot of ways it knows as much as the mind. The intuition—that's what Chris is using. Why has it lost caché in this culture? Why *isn't* it important?"

"Because it's not reliable, and you know it."

"Oh, come on. Modern medicine is 'scientific,' right? Certainly rational. Remember how it used to be healthy to eat steak, and now it'll kill you? They used to bleed you and use leeches on you, and then all that stuff was primitive, and now they're doing it again. You want reliable, don't depend on science."

"Julio, this is crazy! You sound like somebody who lives in Berkeley."

"Well, I'm somebody who spends a lot of my time underwater, and let me tell you, it'll make a believer out of you, Babe."

"A believer in what? God? Is that what you're saying?"

"Not the bearded dude on the mountain. I mean, I guess I'm a Catholic, I don't even know. But not that.

Something else. Something primal. Something about nature itself.''

"Nature?" I don't know why I was so surprised—I was talking to a man whose career was fish. "Jesus Christ, I don't believe it, Julio. You're not from Berkeley, you're straight out of Robert Bly. Next you're going to tell me you came to this realization by painting your face and beating a drum out in the woods.''

He gave me a smile that could have made him a zillion dollars in Hollywood. "What's wrong with that?''

"What's wrong with that? It's stupid, that's what's wrong with it.''

"What's stupid about it?''

"Stupid people do it. Airheads.''

"You mean people who don't think 'rational' is synonymous with pure and decent.''

"Like I said, stupid people." I think I should say here that there was an element of joking in this—I was getting punchy by this time—but there was also a big part of me that truly believed this, and Julio knew it.

"Well, that's me, then.''

"Oh, come on.''

"I mean it.''

"Are you telling me you'd go on a men's weekend? That I'd like to see." (Actually, I would have liked to see him naked except for a few feathers, his face and body painted—when I thought of it that way, my heart speeded up.)

"I'm telling you I've been.''

"What?" I said again.

"Hang on to your hat. That's not the end of it. I'm a member of a men's drumming circle. That's where I've been tonight—want me to prove it? I left my drum in the car.''

"Holy shit.''

"Yes, we of the men's movement feel that way. If it's of the earth, it's holy, shit included."

"Julio, not you. I can't take it." I was holding my face in my hands, rocking back and forth.

He was laughing like a loon. "Rebecca, you are the silliest woman I ever met, you know that?"

I don't know how I knew—perhaps by one of those nonrational methods of Julio's—but I was suddenly aware of a deep trust between the two of us that I hadn't had a clue about. He'd told me his deepest secret, and even as I was telling him I couldn't take it, I was aware how much I loved him for it—for telling me and knowing it wouldn't make a particle of difference to me. Because I was just realizing it didn't—the same way Chris's confession didn't change the way I felt about her.

Julio had called it a few minutes ago—what was changing was the way I viewed the world. The downside was, it was against my will, my better judgment, probably nature, and undoubtedly the law.

I said, "Has everybody in the world got some fucking horrible skeleton in the closet?"

He was falling on the floor laughing.

"Oh, can it. I'm not that cute when I'm mad."

"Yes, you are."

CHAPTER
9

I stayed the night and got up early to drive back—no problem since Kruzick had canceled all my appointments. And as I was saying good-bye to Julio, having climbed into my Jeep so that I towered above him, he stood on tiptoe and got me to bend toward him so he could whisper something. "I was just kidding last night. I'm not really in a drumming circle."

I was outraged. "You shit!"

"Or maybe I'm kidding now."

So if he didn't have a secret before, he had one now— I had no idea if he was or wasn't in the men's movement. And I still had my secret. I hadn't even slightly felt like bringing up such a downer as the big C, but at least he'd distracted me from it.

At the moment I was deeply in love with him. We'd made love after he'd mocked me to his heart's content (and convinced me I deserved it), and in the afterglow I thought back to what he said about the body being as important as the mind, and said to him that surely there couldn't be a higher truth than this. As further proof (if any is needed) that men are less sentimental than women, he'd just laughed and said that was the sort of thinking that got people into trouble. At first I was pissed that he wasn't as carried away by the moment as I was, but I knew he was right. It was the proper blend of truths that we strove for and could never get right. Damn him for being so alert at such a moment.

Yet, what a man. Rob seemed so distant and cold compared to him. So obsessed with the trivia of being a star reporter while Julio was a virtual merman, swimming with the fish and seals, exploring the ocean, flowing with nature. It was such a terribly romantic concept. Yet what would my life be in Monterey? And in San Francisco he'd have no life at all. It was like the movie *Splash*—interspecies love.

Rob was sitting in my office when I got there, obsessed as usual, annoyed that I was an hour late, and hot to get going. Chris, said Kruzick, was in court. Afterward, she was going to go over to the *Chron* and read some more clips.

Rob said, "Could we get going, Rebecca? We've got an appointment with Tommy La Barre in half an hour."

"You actually made an appointment with him?"

"Sure. Saturday night."

I realized I was so sure he was the killer I hadn't thought of confronting him directly.

We saw him at Dante's, a marvel of high-tech black-and-white sophistication that managed to convey—I can't think how—that this was the very zenith of *Italian* high-tech sophistication. And that it had cost roughly three smidgens more than the Giotto doors in Florence. He was drinking Pellegrino at the black marble bar, under a light fixture of cutting-edge simplicity. The sleeves of his white starched shirt were rolled to exactly the same spot on both arms, as if arranged by a well-trained robot. He was just under six feet, about five-ten I'd guess, and thick, a heavy man, so that he looked shorter than he was. He was a blond, and slightly ruddy, his haircut procured, no doubt, at the same place the light fixture had come from—I couldn't have said why, but I had no doubt it had been designed within the last twenty-four hours by the top hairdresser in Milan. It was a wet-look kind of thing, combed off the face, and it would have been a great deal more attractive on a teenage musician. Tommy looked like the sort who said, What's shakin', Babe? when he met a new woman.

But he said it was nice to meet me like anyone else and accompanied the sentiment with a smile that rose to his eyes, not one of those frozen half-face facsimiles so many of my colleagues affected. "Man, I'm in lousy shape," he said. "I miss that guy like a bastard. I *loved* that crazy dude."

"How did you meet him?"

"Hell, I called him up. I said I liked his stuff and why didn't he come in and have dinner on me. He said he couldn't do that, something about newspaper ethics. I didn't get it, but that's what he said. But one day he dropped by for lunch and introduced himself and we hit it off." He shrugged. "The rest is history, as they say."

I would have loved to know the details of that history. Had Tommy given him a little tour of the place, including the infamous private dining rooms? Had one thing led to another until Jason knew way too much for a member of the press?

"He came back again and I sent something over—maybe champagne, I can't remember—and then he kept coming, and I always sent something special for his lady friends. Man, he had a lot of them."

"Did you know his assistant, Adrienne?"

He shrugged. "Who knows? Guy had a different woman every week."

"How about Sarah Byers?"

"Good-looking redhead?"

"No. A plain-looking woman; a little on the frumpy side."

"No way. That wasn't Jase's style at all. Now, me, I don't go for flash." He gave me a very sincere look, as if to say, You'd do just fine, which made me hate him. I've never been one for left-handed compliments. "Jeez, I miss that guy!"

"Why?" I said.

"Why? He was my friend."

"I mean, what did you like about him?"

"He was so damn funny. He was just so damn *quick*, he could have you on the floor in thirty seconds. And he was generous. Best friend you could ever have. Stood by me through"—he got a faraway look—"everything."

"Well, look, you knew him better than just about anyone, right?"

He looked surprised. "Hell, I don't know. I don't know who his other friends were. I mean, except for everybody in town."

"Still, you must have an opinion on what happened. Who'd want to kill a guy like that?"

It was obviously the question he'd been waiting to answer. He sat up perfectly straight and gave Rob a steely gaze—this was man talk. "Know what I think? Know what I really think? I think it was some babe."

"Ah."

"Guy just had too many of 'em for something not to go wrong. Know what I mean?" He kept staring at Rob. "Know what I mean?"

"Just playing the odds," said Rob.

"Yeah. Yeah! Just playing the odds. Some babe did him." He finished off his Pellegrino in one draught. "Did you ever see *Play Misty for Me*? Something like that could have happened. Jason was a public figure; women got crushes on him. I've seen it happen myself." He swept an arm around the room. "Here. Waitresses. Women having dinner, sending him drinks and things. Maybe one of 'em was nuts, maybe she imagined a romance that wasn't there. . . ."

"You know, a funny thing," I said. "We've talked to some of his girlfriends. They say he wasn't sexually involved with them."

"You mean he wasn't sleepin' with 'em? Shit, I'm glad to hear it. I was thinkin' maybe he was Superman or something." He got the faraway look again. "There was a lady in here one night—regular customer—and she sent him her card. She wrote something on it, I never knew what, the waiter didn't look, and he asked me about her. Wanted to know what I thought of her."

I didn't see the relevance. "Did he go out with her?"

"That's not the point. Point is, she was a pro. I'm tellin' you this because, why'd a guy like Jason need a pro? You have to ask yourself. Maybe there's something there for you. That's why I'm tellin' you." He had such a sheepish look on his face that I could only imagine he was speaking so sharply against his better judgment he could hardly get the words out—either that, or it was what we were supposed to think.

"I know this babe. She's in here a lot. I can spot a pro when I see one."

That I believed.

"We could talk to her," said Rob and shrugged, as if it was an awful imposition. But he'd do it for his pal, Tommy. "You know how to reach her?"

He got up off his bar stool and lumbered behind the bar. "Sure. I've got her card somewhere."

He rummaged and gave it to Rob, who glanced at it, thanked him, and slipped it in his pocket. Thinking of Rob's performance in retrospect makes me want to take a vow never to trust anyone, no matter how sincere they seem. It was one of the best acting jobs I've ever seen. Because there was no way in hell to begin to guess how Rob inwardly exulted when he saw the name on that card.

He stayed cool, nattering on about one thing and another, until we got to the car, and then he passed the card to me without a word or a blink.

I let out a shriek, but he already had his ears covered.

The name on the card was that of Elena Mooney, a dear friend of mine. Tommy had been right about one thing, or sort of right—Elena was a pro of sorts. She didn't turn tricks anymore, but she was the classiest madame in town. I'd met her when I was the lawyer for HUENA, the hookers' union, which was now defunct, but Elena and I still had lunch occasionally. For some reason, we'd hit it off.

I phoned to make sure she was up, but someone had beat us to it. "Tommy just called and said you were on your way. Can't wait to see you, Babe. Listen, I'm starving—could you pick up something for lunch? I'll make it, I'll pay for it. All you have to do is get it."

"Sure."

"Oh, Rob's with you, isn't he? Not pasta puttanesca, okay? I know the man's sense of humor."

Since we figured she'd be more in a breakfast mood than otherwise, we got bagels and lox and found we'd guessed right. She was pouring her second cup of coffee when we got there. She sat down at the round table, looking a little bleary with no makeup. She had on short black leggings, pedal-pusher length, and a white T-shirt with whales and dolphins swimming in a blue circle on the front. Her feet were bare, her hair pinned up carelessly, her nails red daggers, as always.

Elena lived in a genuine bordello, with red-flocked walls, bead curtains, the whole schmeer, but the kitchen was like anyone else's, and I knew it almost as well as my own. So I toasted bagels while she talked.

"Tommy's an asshole, isn't he? God! This business you meet people make your skin crawl."

"You're talking like an Elmore Leonard character."

"Lose half my words before breakfast. Blood sugar's down—bagel'll fix me up."

"He says you sent Jason McKendrick your card one night in the restaurant."

"Oh, sure. Like I've got nothing better to do than hang out in that inferno of his. You ever know me to solicit, Rebecca? I ask you! The man offends my dignity."

"Tommy."

"Tommy. Of course. I never even met Jason. He called up, asked if I had anybody for a friend of his. She had to call him, he was shy. Well, no problem— 'nother hundred bucks, that's all. Rob, off the record? You know that, right?"

He spread his hands, all innocence. "Hey, Elena, you know me."

"Thassa prob'em."

I thrust a bagel in front of her. "Eat something, Elena. Now you're losing letters."

She spread cream cheese thickly and applied a good portion of lox while I got bagels ready for Rob and me. He found us a couple of diet Cokes. "The girls are into those," Elena said. "Think they're bad for the complexion, myself."

When she had eaten enough to get her blood sugar up, I said, "So who'd you get for McKendrick?"

"Well, I can't tell you. I mean it, not even you, Rebecca."

"Hey, come on, Elena, this is murder. We need to talk to her."

"You can't. She moved to Alaska last month."

"Okay, she didn't kill him, anyway. But last I heard they had phones there."

"No dice. Look, you want to know two things, right? Did she do it, and did anything happen that might shed some light on anything."

I nodded; Rob chewed.

"Well, no to both questions. He couldn't even get it up."

"What?" Both of us nearly leapt across the table.

She smiled like the Mona Lisa, enjoying the effect she'd created. "Ha. Got you, didn't I? Yeah, she was thrilled. He wanted her to get all dressed up and meet him in this hotel suite. Very, very fancy hotel, I won't say which one. Ordered room service, anything she wanted. Champagne, every kind of thing. She didn't want to drink on duty, but he insisted. Paid her extra. And then he made out with her awhile." She grimaced. "Ick. You know how whores hate to kiss. But he paid her for that, too. I think he took all her clothes off and everything. But he never did fuck her."

"Just didn't? Or tried and couldn't?"

"Well, just wouldn't, I think."

"But you're not sure."

"Oh, okay, okay. I'm ornery before brunch. We'll call her, okay? Will that make you happy?" And she left to get a cordless phone.

Pretty soon we were talking to one Claudia (aka Tami) Robinson, who said she couldn't remember that much about it, because after all she'd been drinking, but to the best of her recollection, Mr. McKendrick had kept his clothes on.

"What was that all about?" I asked.

"Who knows? You get weirdos."

"McKendrick was a weirdo?"

"Does that sound normal to you?"

"Did he give any reason for it?"

"He said he just wanted to be with me and hold me.
In case you don't know the technical jargon, that's what
they say when they can't get it up."

"Did he do or say anything odd—I mean, except for
that?"

She thought for a minute. "Yeah. Yeah, he did. He
cried."

"He cried?"

"Yeah. He held me and cried all over me. I remember, I said to Elena, 'Hey, you can't get AIDS from
tears, can you?' I mean, they're bodily fluids. But, anyway, he called me a name."

I stiffened, ready for a particularly nasty obscenity.
"What did he call you?"

"Sean. He called me Sean. He said, 'Oh, Sean, I'm
so sorry.' "

"Did he say who Sean was?"

"Look, all I wanted to do was get out of there. You
think I asked? The guy was drunk and sloppy. No wonder he couldn't get it up—nobody could have."

"Okay, just one more thing. Did he pay for a whole
night?"

"Yeah, by the time you added in all the extras—
kissing and drinking and everything—oh, yeah, and me
calling him. Then there was the suite and the champagne and dinner and everything. Jesus! Must have been
about a fifteen-hundred dollar night for him."

If he'd made a habit of this sort of thing, that would
explain where his money went.

CHAPTER
10

Tami swore she hadn't ever told any of this to a soul ("I mean, why would I? Just who would you expect to give a shit?") so we had to figure Tommy La Barre hadn't known when he sent us over there. But what I couldn't figure was why he sent us. I still thought he was our man.

"So do I," said Rob. "But we can't afford to ignore this Sean thing."

"Okay. You've got to go help Chris plow through clips anyway. Why don't you look for any Seans he might have panned while you're at it. And I'll call back everyone we've already talked to and see if they know what it means."

So we did—and turned up nothing.

The only good news was, I got in nearly five hours' work on my pending case before it was time to pop over to Mickey and Alan's. Kruzick had left, as usual, at five—"got to go pluck that pheasant"—leaving me to slave for two more hours. But somehow it wasn't pheasant I smelled when I walked in—it was pasta puttanesca, and I guess it was just that kind of day.

I inspected the kittens and returned to the kitchen just in time for the ceremonial unveiling of the garlic bread. Mickey said, "I made pasta because it's your security food," which was so sweet I didn't remind her it was

105

all she ever made. Kruzick bore the salad to the table
in triumph, and I found myself hungry as a horse.

But I could barely eat because Mickey wanted details—lots of them. Kruzick had told her very little,
saying I was coming over, she might as well get it from
me. But of course he wouldn't even have known about
some of the things I wanted to talk about.

It was just as well because I needed new eyes to look
at this thing. The task, as I saw it, was to keep my law
partner out of jail. I couldn't see a way to do that without finding the murderer. Was I right so far?

They nodded.

Well, then, what to do now? Look for Jason's enemies? I hadn't found any. Look for Chris's? She claimed
she didn't have any unless you counted Tommy La
Barre. Was he a good suspect?

Vigorous nods. Shouts of approval. Tommy had fans.

So how to find a motive?

"Well, you could start in on his friends," said
Mickey.

I sighed. "I can't go around doing that—I mean, I'm
still a lawyer. I guess I better hire an investigator."

"But you promised Rob."

It was true. We were still using the *Chronicle*'s resources; I could hardly stop now.

Kruzick said, "Maybe you could go to gay bars and
ask around for Sean."

I almost said, "Maybe I'll send you," but that would
have been playing right into his hands. He would have
launched into an offensive swish act if I had. Years of
knowing Kruzick were finally paying off.

"Or you could thend me," he said, holding his hands
like paws, so I could watch his wrists go limp. So much
for heading him off at the pass.

"We could thend you to your room," Mickey said.

"But theriously," said Alan.

"Go!" Mickey pointed. She was getting tough, and I liked it.

"I didn't mean to do that. Seriously. Listen, I want to say something."

We cocked our heads politely.

"This guy's sex life is weird. I mean, it's a trail to follow. It's too strange to leave it alone."

He was right. It might have nothing to do with anything, but we couldn't just leave it.

"And I've got this other idea. Maybe some witch is mad at Chris. You know, like Chris is more powerful than she is, so she puts a spell on her to get revenge."

I tried to fathom this. "You know about her being psychic?"

I know she's into something from the phone calls she gets.

Mickey said, "It would take a pretty damn powerful witch to get her name and number in Jason's pocket."

"It's interesting," I said, "the way everybody went right from psychic to magic."

"What?"

"Look. We've got to take Chris seriously. She feels lousy about being psychic. Let's not make fun of her, okay?"

"Touch-y," said Kruzick.

But Mickey said, "What's it all about, anyway? I mean, it is pretty weird."

It seemed the secret was out. So I told them what Chris had told me in the dim sum restaurant. And then I launched into my favorite new subject—poor Rebecca betrayed by a heartless world that wouldn't be still: "It's hard for me, getting used to this. I mean, my best friend really isn't the person I thought she was. She's actually been leading a double life when you get down to it. I said that to Julio and turned out he had, too—I mean not really, he's just in the men's movement—or maybe he really isn't, I don't—"

"Excuse me." Mickey was up and out of there. We heard a door slam.

"What's going on?"

Kruzick shrugged. "Hell if I know."

I got up and followed, but Mickey had locked herself in the bedroom. I heard sobs, but she wouldn't answer my knocks. I couldn't get back to the dining room fast enough—almost tripped over Lulu in the process.

"Alan, *what* is going on?"

"On the rag, I guess. She's been weird lately." He started clearing the table. That way he didn't have to meet my eyes.

"I swear to God, if you do not treat my sister the way she deserves to be treated, I'll—"

"What? Fire me? Hey, I quit. But I *am* treating her right. Why the hell is this my fault?"

"Fire you! I'll grind you up and make you into hot dogs, which I will donate to the zoo with the stipulation that they be fed to the monkeys. Mess with her and you are monkey shit, Kruzick!"

"You need a vacation, you know that? And take Mickey with you."

Sure. Take her with me. He wanted to get her out of the house so he could carry on his affair. It had to be that because what else would she get so upset about the minute you mentioned secret lives?

Figuring I was momentarily superfluous, I got out of there.

And found myself with the same old blues I'd been singing all weekend. I didn't want to be alone, that was all. It wasn't like me, but I couldn't shake it. Not even, apparently, by knocking on the door of everyone I knew.

Why was I feeling so damned insecure? Honestly, it was a full two minutes, while my mind went through a litany of trivialities, before I remembered the lump. With amazement, I realized I'd had all day to call a doctor, and I hadn't done it. Nothing like putting bad news off till tomorrow.

But it was more than that—just as neurotic, but more. I couldn't take time out to be sick right now. I could only deal with one crisis at a time—and not only that, I didn't physically have the time. As rationalizations went, it worked. Besides, everybody else seemed to have a secret right now. Surely I was entitled to one.

I went home and played the piano and thought about what Chris had said—about the way people mock other people, about orthodoxy and the way it's kept pristine. Some things you just didn't question and others were fair game. I had asked my father once, when I was a little girl, why God was a man, and he had said, "He isn't a man; he's a spirit."

"But why is he a man spirit?" I asked.

And my dad had said, "Because that's the way God made himself."

You know what? I'd never bought it. But you just didn't go around talking that way.

I'd never understood the word "spiritual"; didn't have the least idea what it meant. Nor, I gathered, did most people like me—the kind Chris said made fun of other people's beliefs. I wondered if that was because it was just so damned hard to buy some of the sacred cows— but you had to bow down to them anyway.

Did this mean I had a religious secret myself? I love it, I thought to myself—the Shirley MacLaine of Green Street.

Frankly, the closest I can get to a spiritual experience is playing music. I played Scarlatti and felt better.

* * *

On Tuesday, Chris and I had a breakfast date at my apartment to take stock—not my idea. Such things never are, but she's a morning person. Nonetheless, she arrived as haggard and drawn as if she'd had an argument with a controlled substance.

"You poor peach," I said, stealing her favorite word. "Are you okay?"

"Still not over the weekend, I guess." But she smiled as if she was merely tired from dancing all night. She'd bounce back, but it would take time. Time, and renewed self-esteem—the vindication of turning the real killer over to Martinez. I wanted to give her that with every cell in my body.

She stretched out her lanky body on one of my facing white couches, in perfect confidence that coffee would arrive soon. It did, of course.

I took the opposite sofa.

Quickly, we brought each other up to date. She hadn't found anything in the clips. Tommy La Barre was looking better and better.

"But let's go over everybody again," I said. The question of enemies was touchy—who wanted to think someone didn't like her? And Chris was Southern. "We're s'posd to be like golden retrievers," she used to say. "Born to please."

"Have you ever been responsible for someone going to jail?"

"Hey, partner, we're defense attorneys. Did you forget?"

"Okay, okay. Wasn't there anyone—like maybe from high school or something—that you broke up with before they were ready?"

"I never even *dated* in high school."

I wouldn't want to say her mood was negative, but

she didn't really resemble a golden retriever. I brought in some pastries from my local Italian bakery, but she didn't reach for one. A bad sign.

"Well, look," I said. "I really don't mean to criticize your friends, but you've got to admit the Raiders of the Lost Art aren't exactly out of *Our Town*. I mean, nothing against being psychic and all, but they're a little on the strange side, and I was just wondering—"

To my amazement, something struck her funny. "You are such a peachblossom!" she said, and it was the closest she'd sounded to her old self for nearly a week. "You're tryin' *so* hard to be nice. I guess I really got you with that lecture on tolerance. I'm sorry. Really. I was just in a mood."

"Actually, it gave me a lot to think about. Especially when Julio confessed he's in the men's movement."

That provoked a new outburst of gales. "The men's movement! Come *on*!"

"Hey, what happened to tolerance and not making fun of people just because they're different?"

"Julio as the wild man. I can't stand it." She was out of control.

"Hey, look, he's got a right—"

"To paint his *face*? Rebecca, there's such a thing as taste."

These ever-changing Chrises—one all urban scorn, the other put-upon minority—were starting to get to me. "Chris, you're making me mad."

"Mad? Huh? What'd I say?"

"If you want to be taken seriously, you'd better take other people seriously."

She sat up—she can drink coffee lying down, and that was what she'd been doing. "Don't get mad at me. Listen, I really need you."

"Well, look, it doesn't make sense. You're leading

some secret life with a bunch of screwballs from the space bar in *Star Wars*, and you think it's okay to laugh at some gorgeous hunk who's trying to get in touch with his manhood.''

Which just showed how shell-shocked I was. I would have taken his announcement a lot more in the vein she had if she hadn't been such a little trailblazer.

"Well, I mean! *Julio*. Who wouldn't like to get in touch with his manhood?" She laughed a little more and wiped her eyes. "I'm sorry, I guess it was the thought of him naked. I must have felt like dwelling on it.''

"He's too short for you."

"Anyway, about the *Star Wars* cast—begging your pardon, but they're the only ones who couldn't have killed Jason. I was with them, remember?"

"Oh, yeah." I thought a minute. Maybe I was still a little mad with her, maybe just emboldened by her giggle fit. Before I could stop the words, I said, "Well, goddammit, if you're so psychic, why don't you know who did it?"

"It's not that easy."

I fixed her with a stern eye. "Keep talking."

"The stuff's not all that reliable."

"How does it work, anyway?"

"You have to know what questions to ask, for one thing."

"How about this one: 'Did Tommy La Barre kill Jason McKendrick?' ''

She shrugged. "Why the hell not?" She closed her eyes and dropped her chin. When she opened her eyes, she looked amazed. "Well, he might not have. I didn't think I'd get anything, because it's impossible to read for yourself. But I did get a little something. It looked a lot like 'innocent.' ''

"Does it come in images or what?"

"Sometimes. I get lights mostly. Tommy just didn't light up over that one."

"Where do you think it's coming from? Are you reading his mind or what?"

"I wish to hell I knew." For a moment she looked as miserable as when she'd first told me about it.

"Well, back to the original subject."

"Who hates me."

"Look, somebody had to know you were in that group. They had to steal your car, remember?"

"They just followed me. I'm sure that was all it was."

"Even so. You can't get around the fact they went to a lot of trouble to frame you. If it wasn't Tommy La Barre, who? Who, who, who?"

"I'm getting depressed."

"You've got to face it, Chris. Somebody wanted you to take the rap for murder. That's a lot of animosity."

"I'm getting depressed again. Can't we get Julio to come do a naked dance for us?"

I didn't answer.

Finally, she said, "Maybe it was a crazy person."

"Do you know any?"

"Well, La Barre didn't act normal that time when he threatened me, but now that I think of it, you know what? I'll bet he was doing a lot of coke at the time. I wonder if he still is."

"If so, that would qualify him as crazy."

"He might be the only one I know. But you know one, of course—the Cosmic Blind Date."

"Oh. Roger DeCampo. But it can't be him—he doesn't know you. La Barre suggested Jason might have attracted one—like in *Play Misty for Me*."

"But it would still have to be somebody who knows me too."

Good. She'd accepted that. Suddenly I said, "Have you ever heard of a Sarah Byers?"

"No. Why?"

"Oh. I thought for a minute I might be onto something."

"You know, now that I think of it, it had to be somebody who knew something about stealing cars—they must have had a slim jim, and they must have known how to hot-wire."

"Sounds right."

"But I don't know anybody like that."

I was quiet, trying to think where to go from here. Finally Chris said, "I wonder if I should try something."

"What?"

"You'll think it's crazy, but I don't know, it couldn't hurt."

"What, for Christ's sake?"

"Maybe I could get the group together."

"Group?" I was drawing a blank.

"You know. The Raiders. Maybe we could come up with something."

She was right. It couldn't hurt.

CHAPTER
11

Chris was taking the morning off, still going through clips, but I could allow myself no such luxury. I *had* to get some work done, or that was the way it felt before I got to the office. Once ensconced, I found very nearly all I could do was fret. I picked up the phone to call the doctor, and before I'd dialed, I'd convinced myself I was making a fool of myself. There was really no lump, I'd turned into one of those people doctors call crocks.

I called Mickey. "Are you okay?"

"Listen, I'm really sorry about last night. I was about to call you."

"Was it something I said?"

"Are you free for lunch?"

I looked at my watch—not really. But I said, "If we could do a quick one. Sandwiches in the park or something."

"Perfect. How about Embarcadero Plaza? Could you get the sandwiches, do you think?"

I sighed. My life was going this way lately. "Okay. But you didn't answer the question. Are you okay or not?"

"Things are a little weird."

I sighed again, feeling like somebody's grandmother.

"Well, how about you? You sound depressed."

"I'll tell you all about it."

115

I went to the ladies' room and felt my breast. No question: The Thing was there. Panic swept through me, leaving me shaking against the stall door. I had fought a man with a knife once, when I had no weapon at all, and I hadn't felt this kind of fear. This was like the movie *Alien*; when the beast was inside you, when your own body betrayed you, there was nowhere to turn.

I went back and picked up the phone. I got the doctor's office and said I wanted to make an appointment.

"Is this for a checkup, or are you experiencing some problem?"

Why did I have to tell this stranger? It was none of her damn business.

I mustered as much dignity as I could. "I'll tell Carolyn when I see her," I said, using my doctor's first name.

"I'm sorry, our procedure is to find out when we make the appointment."

"Just like your procedure is to weigh me when I come in whether I want to be weighed or not."

The woman's voice was frosty. "We need to know whether you've had a sudden change in weight."

"You know, I really can't—" But before I got any further Kruzick stuck his head in my door. If it was none of the receptionist's business, it was most assuredly none of his. I was suddenly so embarrassed, the woman was spared the lecture I'd been about to deliver on doctors treating patients like children, infantilizing us and making rules for their convenience rather than our comfort. Rules, hell! I might have shouted, I'm *hiring* this woman, and I'm the one paying the bills. From now on, *I* make the rules.

I could kill Kruzick. Think how satisfying that would have been. Instead I just asked to have Carolyn call me back.

My secretary assumed a prissy mouth. "Shall I hold madame's calls today?"

"Let me talk to Rob if he calls, and Carolyn."

"And who might Carolyn be?"

"That might be none of your beeswax."

"Veddy good, mum." I kind of liked him in this role, but if I said so he'd think of a way to make it irritating; in his way, the man was a genius.

When he had gone, I stared into space awhile, trying to orient myself. I was a wreck this morning, either from the fear or from the stress of living in denial for three days. Or was it only two? I couldn't even count anymore. What it felt like that morning was the last day of Pompeii—something awful was going to happen, something cataclysmic. I got out my calendar and looked at it—sure enough it was two days before my period. Throw hormones in with the rest, and you had a major paranoia attack.

Rationally, that should have explained it, should have calmed me. I should have been able to say to myself, "I'm doing what I can for Chris and also my lump, and that's the end of it." But I guess Julio was right about the mind being less important than we think. I couldn't get a grip.

Just to have something to do with my sweaty hands, I called Sarah Byers's number, hoping for a referral to her office. Instead, I got this: "This is Sarah. Don't ask for whom the bell tolls. It tolls for me."

God. Was that a suicide message or just a reference to ringing telephones? It gave me the creeps.

After that, with Kruzick holding my calls, I had no choice but to work. I ended up so involved I was surprised when he came in, announced he was going to lunch, and dumped a stack of message slips on my desk. The top one nearly sent me through the ceiling.

"Alan, I thought I told you to put Carolyn through."

"And so I would have, Mum, if the lady had called."

"She did call." I showed him the message slip. "And by the way, the butler act's wearing thin."

Without batting an eye, he changed to Southern ditherer: "Well, I declare to goodness if that doesn't say 'Dr. Perlmutter.' You don't s'pose we had a l'il ol' failyah of communication, do you?"

"Oh, go to lunch." I called Carolyn back, told the damn receptionist I had a lump, and made an appointment.

I was fifteen minutes late meeting Mickey as a result. No problem—she didn't turn up for another five.

I handed her a tuna sandwich and didn't even let her get it unwrapped. "So let's have it. Kruzick's cheating on you, isn't he?"

"No. It's nothing to do with Alan. Exactly."

"Well, what then?"

"I'm the one who's having an affair."

"You! But, Mickey—" I couldn't say what came to mind: *My baby sister is an angel; she doesn't do things like that.*

"I'm pond scum, right?"

"Of course not. But what's going on?"

"It's a friend of Alan's. A guy from the theater. He's married and has three kids. The youngest is eight months old."

"Gosh." That was the best I could do. I was as close to speechless as I get.

"Pretty bad, huh?"

"Um. May I be perfectly honest? Not good. But like I said—what's going on?"

"I don't know." The words came out in a whisper. She said it again: "I don't know. I think I'm in love with two people at once."

"You're in love with this guy?" I was so surprised I practically shouted it.

Her eyes filled up. "You don't know. You just don't know how awful it is."

"I guess I don't. How is it awful?"

"Oh God, the guilt. And being jealous of his wife and children. And never seeing him enough. And knowing I'd die if Alan found out . . . You just don't know!"

The solution seemed simple enough to one who wasn't in the middle of it. The question was whether to mention it. I tried to make a delicate little joke of it: "Well. Usually one man . . ."

"Oh, stop! Rebecca, you just can't know what this is like."

"I'm sorry. I didn't mean to moralize."

"It's okay."

"What are you going to do?"

"I don't know. Oh God, how could I have not mentioned the indecision? That's the worst part."

"Is it a question of leaving Alan and being with this man?"

"Sometimes I think so, and sometimes it just seems preposterous. I don't know anything anymore."

I wasn't used to my little sister as a drama queen. She was usually so sensible—unless you counted the astonishing lapse of judgment that had prompted her to pick Kruzick. I found I wasn't crazy about being a party to this thing, either—it seemed wildly self-destructive, not to mention unfair to the man's family. I had a thing about married men who had affairs—meaning I found them beneath contempt. I didn't at all know how to deal with this. But then, what else was new this week?

I told Mickey things like I was there for her and to

let me know if there was anything I could do (as if someone had died) and didn't even mention The Thing.

On the whole I was glad we'd decided on lunch outside. I needed the walk back to clear my head. I thought about consulting an astrologer—surely the stars must be causing all the chaos; it seemed impossible that mere human beings could be responsible.

Chris came in, calling first to make sure Curry and Martinez weren't around, and between the two of us we made the place look a lot like a law office for a few hours.

Rob turned up around three. "I spent the day checking out Tommy La Barre. Bad news: he was at the restaurant at eight-thirty the night of the murder. Eight-thirty and all night. Two nights a week he acts as maitre d' himself, and that was one of them. The night was one of the busiest they've had lately, and he was hopping every second—no way in hell he could have slipped out and done the deed."

"A guy like Tommy La Barre could have hired somebody," said Chris.

"I've been thinking about his giving us Elena's card. We know McKendrick saw Tami, right? But that doesn't prove he didn't also have a scene in one of Tommy's party rooms. Tommy could have done it to distract us. Rob, listen—is this possible? Maybe McKendrick was just pretending to be friends with La Barre; maybe the whole point was to get a story."

Rob shook his head. "He'd have had to work with an editor on it—and that person would have put two and two together by now and mentioned it. But the other part of the theory's still good—let's don't count him out. Meanwhile, I don't know what to do about the Sean thing; I can't seem to turn up anything. However"—he paused for effect—"not to worry, because the whole thing might be solved. Two new leads—after you left, Chris, I kept looking through the clips, thinking I might run across a Sean. I didn't, but I found someone McKendrick panned who had access to your car keys; someone who could as easily have driven your car that night as you.''

Chris and I spoke in unison: "Who?"

''Alan Kruzick.''

''Did I hear those three magic syllables?'' Alan popped in the door, with something in his hand, probably for Chris or me to sign.

''You never mentioned Jason McKendrick panned you.''

''*Streetcar Named Desire.*'' He shrugged. ''So I'm no Brando. Big deal.''

''Yes, but the funny thing is, that was the last play you were in before you came to work here. McKendrick broke your spirit, you realized you'd never make it in this town as an actor, so you threw in the towel and went to work. But you were bitter about it—he'd ruined your life and you decided he had to pay for it. You awaited your opportunity. One day, when Chris left her purse unattended, you took her keys and got a duplicate made of her car key. Then one night you followed her— no, better yet, you followed her a lot—but one night she went to a place very near Jason McKendrick's apartment. You decided to do it that night.''

''I can do better than that,'' said Chris. ''He knew I was going to that group. I told him. Right, Alan?''

Alan said, ''I have the right to remain silent. I am not required to say anything at any time or to answer any questions. Anything I say can be used against me in court. I have the right to talk to a lawyer for advice before being questioned and to have her with me during questioning. If I cannot afford a lawyer . . .''

Chris and I stared at each other. "Will it fly?" she said.

" 'The silence often of pure innocence,'" intoned Alan, "persuades when speaking fails.' "

We ignored him. "It's a little Perry Masonish, but sure—this is it! Rob, you're a genius."

"Well, actually, it was only a theory. Don't you think you're being a little hasty? I mean, who's going to type your letters?"

"Nobody's going to arrest Alan. We'll just use him to point up the preposterousness of suspecting Chris. He had just as much opportunity and a better motive. Alan could even testify. Hey, how about it?"

"Give me liberty or give me death."

"That means yes," I said. "He's never going to turn down a role like that."

"Wait a minute," said Kruzick. "How did I get her name and address into his pocket?"

"Oh, don't worry. We'll think of something. Or maybe we just won't mention it. Do you have an alibi for that night?"

"I was with—uh, no, come to think of it. Mickey wasn't home that night."

"Fabulous." Chris was beaming.

It was at least a better theory than Martinez and Curry had. I planned to give it to them first thing in the morning; maybe it would head them off at the pass.

Rob said, "There's one more thing. I got a call from a woman who says she knows who killed him."

CHAPTER 12

Her name was Hilary Winterhalter, and Rob had arranged for us to see her at six-thirty that night. But he didn't say much else about her, only that she sounded a little hysterical, as if she could be the crazy fan Tommy La Barre had postulated. Afterward, I thought, would be a good time to call on Sarah Byers.

Chris waited for Rob to leave and said that was fine but not to make any plans for Wednesday, the next night—it was the regular meeting of the Raiders of the Lost Art, and Chris had had a little talk with Rosalie. They were going to work on the murder, and I was welcome to sit in.

I was interested. I was starting to wonder if Chris had gotten "innocent" off Tommy La Barre because he'd hired someone rather than done the deed himself. Now that that idea had come up, maybe the Raiders could tell us if it was a productive direction.

Did I mean that? Was that me thinking that?

Well, anyway, I'd keep an open mind.

That night I drove. Unlike Julio, Rob liked my Jeep—liked riding up high like I did. We'd decided to treat ourselves even though it was a high-profile car for this kind of thing.

Hilary had a ground-floor flat in Bernal Heights with a little porch outside where she was waiting. She was

a very small girl and, if the truth be told, no one you'd
pick out of a crowd. Nature had been stingy with
her, given her tiny features, including a pointy little
chin, sallow skin, and thin hair. But she had good taste.
"Oooh. Great car," she said before we were even
parked. "Jason's car was such an old wreck." Which
made us both sigh with relief—Rob hadn't been sure
she'd really known him, that she wasn't just some nut
who read the paper.

Introductions over, she led us into a pleasant enough
room, furnished with Pier One wicker and dhurrie rugs.
A cheap white desk shone pristine, as if it was never
used. An overhead light was only a paper lantern covering a bare bulb. A poster of the Golden Gate Bridge,
one I'd seen at a thousand tourist shops, was tacked to
a wall. The stark effect would have benefited by a few
plants, but Hilary seemed to favor fauna instead. There
was a small animal in a cage, a hamster, I thought, and
a handsome golden Lab curled up on one of the rugs.

"Do you mind dogs? Jason hated them."

"Of course not," I said, and dropped to my knees
to pet the Lab. "Hi, fella; what a lovely boy! What a
nice boy! What's your name?" The usual baby talk.

"She's called Goldie Hawn, actually. But it's nice of
you to notice her." She sighed. "Jason made me lock
her up or he wouldn't come over."

"He sounds difficult."

"Oh, no. He was really fun. He could make me laugh
all night. I mean all evening—he never stayed the
night." She sat down, gesturing for us to do the same.

"The two of you dated?"

"Well, I thought we were dating, but now that I think
of it, we didn't go out much. He'd just come over
and"—she stared out the window, avoiding eye contact—"fuck me."

Everything she said indicated she was furious with him. Rob and I exchanged glances: Maybe we were onto something. It seemed best to go slow.

Rob put on his friendly reporter smile. "How'd you meet him?"

"Well, I'm a nurse. He came to the hospital to visit a sick friend." She had tied her thin hair into a sort of low ponytail, which she pulled over her shoulder and stroked as she spoke. The impression was of someone not used to having the spotlight, nervous at being interviewed. You couldn't help wondering what had attracted a man like Jason McKendrick to her—what, in fact, had even made him notice her.

"He sort of started kind of blatantly flirting with me, and I thought he was just another asshole. Married, like all of them. So I didn't respond except to be kind of rude, if you want to know the truth, I guess, and finally he said, 'You don't know who I am, do you?' And I was really afraid I should, like he was somebody that everybody knew but me, and I was really dumb. So I said, 'Hey, you're that guy on Channel Four,' and he and his friend laughed their heads off. I felt so *stupid*. His friend said, 'Hey, Hillie,'—he called me Hillie— 'This is Jason McKendrick you're talking to.' I just said, 'Uh, hello,' and left without even shaking hands I was so embarrassed. Because I'd never even heard of him." She hung her head as if it were the deepest shame of the culture. But when the pointy chin came up, she was angry again.

"How was I supposed to know about somebody like that? I can't afford to go to plays or anything. He thought he was so damned important. Anyway, I was at the nurses' station after that, and I guess he felt bad—that he made me feel bad—so he asked me to have coffee in the cafeteria. And then, the funny thing was we really,

really hit it off. He was so *funny*. I mean, he was just so *funny*. I never met anybody like that in my whole life. And then it turned out he was this big-deal columnist or whatever he was.''

''So you started seeing each other.''

''Um-hm. The first time he asked me for a drink and then we came back here. The second time, he said why didn't he come over and we'd get some Chinese food. And then after that, he'd just kind of call and wait for me to ask him to come over. And then I was supposed to buy this damned expensive Scotch that was all he'd drink. And fuck him. Always on a Monday or a Tuesday night or something. Never a weekend. And stupid me. I didn't even catch on to what was happening.'' She addressed Rob. ''You were his friend, right? I bet you had no idea what a shit he was.''

Rob turned to me, silently appealing for help; I wondered what he did when I wasn't there.

''It certainly sounds like he took advantage,'' I said.

''You bet your ass he did.'' It sounded shocking coming out of such a small, childlike person, the anger behind it seemingly incongruous. ''I was just out of a ten-year marriage—I got married right after high school and never dated anyone but my husband, Joey, and that was in the eleventh grade! I didn't know a thing about men; or dating. Or sex. Well, there are lots of women like me, right?''

''You mean women involved with Jason McKendrick?''

She looked surprised. ''I don't know. Were there?''

''I'm sorry. I guess I didn't understand what you meant—women like you in what way?''

''Dumb. Naive. Just like there's lots of men like Jason McKendrick. Assholes.''

Both Rob and I were silent. Goldie Hawn snored.

"I want everybody to know, that's why I called you. I want people to know what he was really like."

Rob finally summoned the courage to say, "You seem awfully angry."

"He fucked me, he got me pregnant, he dumped me."

I gasped. "Oh, you poor thing. How awful—to go through an abortion alone."

"I didn't have an abortion. Why would I have an abortion? Joey and I had been trying to get pregnant the whole time we were married. Come look." She led us down a hall to a closed door. Inside was a nursery, with a sleeping baby in a crib. For the first time since she'd seen my Jeep, Hilary smiled. "This is Shirleen. Shirleen McKendrick."

"Did Jason help support her?"

"Shhh!" She put her finger to her lips, took us out of the room, and closed the door. She said, "Jason never even came to see her. He said she wasn't his kid."

"Why did he say that?"

She didn't answer till we were back in the living room. "Well, he came over one night, and Joey was here. By the way, you know why I'm telling you this? I want you to know I'm not after any money. I was still married when I was seeing Jason, and Joey came over a couple of times then." She dropped her eyes. "Once we slept together, but I didn't get pregnant. I mean, I'm sure of that. Do you understand?" This time she looked hard at me.

I nodded and said what she was too shy to say: "You mean, you got your period afterward?"

She spoke with eyes still down, a faint blush on her cheeks. "Yes. So I know Shirleen's Jason's—but look, I know I'd look trashy to some judge. I'm not trying to get money. I just don't want other women to have to go through this.''

Somehow I didn't think she'd be canonized for her nobility, but I could see why she'd called Rob. She was furious, and I didn't blame her. However, there was a tiny point we hadn't covered. The time had come.

Rob said, ''Hilary. On the phone, you said you knew who the murderer was.''

''I do. It was someone like me.''

''I beg your pardon?''

''Look, I've got a motive, haven't I? There were times when I'd have liked to kill him, God forgive me. I'm a god-fearing woman, Mr. Burns. I go to church every Sunday and always have. And I still felt like I wanted to kill that man. I know it was wrong, but I did. And I know . . . I just know . . . that that's who did it. Someone like me.''

''But who?''

''Well, I don't know her *name*. I just know her profile. Isn't that how cops catch people—with profiles?''

''Look, Hilary, have you talked to the police about this?''

''No. I wanted to get it in the *paper*; that's why I called *you*.'' She was getting panicky now. It made her whiny.

''If I write about it, the police are going to come calling, and they're probably going to ask you where you were on the night of the murder.''

''I was here! I'm always here. With Shirleen.''

''You weren't with any adults?''

''What does that matter? Shirleen's still nursing—I couldn't leave her alone. That should be obvious to anybody!''

''Hey, Hey, take it easy.''

"Well, whose side are you on, anyway? I think you should go. I think you should both just go."

It was starting to be a very appealing idea. But there was one thing I had to ask. "There's a woman . . ." I hoped she'd think I meant a woman involved with Jason. "Do you know a Chris Nicholson, by any chance?"

She didn't change expression. "I never heard of any Chris Nicholson, and I want you out of my house now."

We left.

"Is that," said Rob, "what they mean by contemporary female rage?"

"I think that's what they mean by a fruitcake."

"She's got a reason to be mad."

"Yes, but she's volatile. That's what's scary about her. Remind me to ask Chris if she could possibly know her."

"At least we finally met someone who says she slept with him."

"Oh, Sarah does, too. I wonder if she's got a baby."

But Sarah had neither baby, dog, nor hamster. She had cats—a round, unmoving calico who could have been the model for T.S. Eliot's Gumby cat, a lithe, quick gray shadow with a whiplike tail, and a pathetic black kitten who reminded me a lot of my first impression of Hilary. I wondered if he had as dark a side as she did.

We'd come unannounced, catching Sarah in the middle of broiling a steak, but she turned it off, said she'd eat later, she was glad to see us, and would we like a drink. Following Rob's rule of thumb, I asked for white wine, he had a gin and tonic, and Sarah went for bourbon and water.

She told us about the cats, one especially. Their names were Melanie, Scarlett, and Jason, the little black one named for Sarah's lost love. She had found him trying to cross the street on Thursday, the day she heard the news of Jason's death, and she had brought him home, feeling superstitious somehow: "I mean, I know he can't really *be* Jason, even if you believe in reincarnation—there wouldn't have been enough time. But it was like he was sent, because Jason wasn't there anymore, to comfort me or something, I don't know. Does that make sense?"

It didn't, but we pretended.

"I couldn't just leave him there, out in the cold." I didn't remind her it was August. "He's such a sweet'ums, aren't you, puss-pot?" The kitten turned tail and ran—right for me. It leapt into my lap, lay down delightedly, and started to purr. Well, I'd wanted more kittens in my life.

"The only thing is, Melanie hates him. I think she might kill him. He really likes you, though. You wouldn't be able to—"

"I have fish." But I was beginning to question the wisdom of choosing pets you could only look at over those that lay in your lap and purred. "Sarah, you were saying the other night that you and Jason had been lovers."

Tears welled in her eyes. "Uh-huh."

"We were hoping you could tell us a little about what he was like. We're having trouble finding people who were really close to him."

"We were so close it was almost scary." She took a long pull of the bourbon.

"But I thought you didn't know his family. His sister, I mean."

"It wasn't that kind of close. It was something spiritual, something you couldn't really name. Just a way of feeling that made all the rest of that stuff unimportant.''

"Oh.'' I tried to remember what she'd said before. "I thought you said you two weren't dating anymore.''

"We weren't. I wasn't . . . I don't think I was *enough*, you know, enough of anything for Jason. I wasn't smart enough, I wasn't pretty enough. I'm just grateful I could be close to him for a little while.'' She drained her glass and went to make herself another drink.

Rob rolled his eyes at me, but I tried not to look at him. I was feeling far too sorry for Sarah to play games behind her back.

"How did you two meet?'' I called out the question while she rattled ice cubes.

She came back, her step light, smiling at the memory—and no doubt at the zing of bourbon in her bloodstream. "It was so romantic. It was the most romantic thing you can imagine. I work over at Books 'n' Stuff, you know? It's a great, great job. I get to meet all these really famous people, like wonderful authors, but usually they're all from out of town. They come in and sign their books and leave. I used to dream that I'd meet somebody who wouldn't even care that we don't live in the same town, he'd just take me away with him. And then this local publisher collected a bunch of essays and things from newspapers, and two of Jason's articles were included. It was such a little book we didn't even have a signing. I mean how would we, anyway?—there were a million authors.

"So one day this really cute guy came in, and he was real shy and everything. He found the book and brought it up to me, real shy. He found a page with one of his articles on it, and he said, 'Could I show you something? This is me.' He sort of turned red about that

time and he said, 'Would you like me to sign your stock
or anything?' I just thought he was adorable.''

She got up to get herself another bourbon, but I was
quite sure more details were coming. This was clearly
a story she loved to tell.

"I really didn't think we were going to sell that many
of the books. But he was just so cute, I couldn't resist.
I acted like we'd really love it if we did that and made
this great big show of putting the books up by the reg-
ister with little stickers that said, 'Autographed
Copy.' ''

"Anyway, we got to talking and kidding around, and
he was so funny—I mean, he had me completely in
stitches. I'd just never met anybody like that. You know,
he was a lot older than me and all—I guess it never
occurred to me that he'd ask me out. But two weeks
later he called. Would you believe he said, 'You probably won't remember me?' Like you'd forget if Mel
Gibson walked into your life one day. I mean, it was
like that.''

"So you started dating."

"Can you believe it? We did. Me, Sarah Byers, and
Jason McKendrick.''

"And where did you go on your dates?"

"Oh, Jason absolutely hated to go out. He just
couldn't *stand* it. You know, that was his whole job—
going out. He said it was the last thing he wanted to do
on a date, so we'd always just stay in. It was wonderful;
really cozy, like we'd known each other forever—and of
course that way we did get to know each other a lot
faster. Something about the setting, I guess. We were
like . . . I don't know, sister and brother, we were so
close. Only I don't really mean that like it sounds—the
sex was just incredible. I've never in my life felt so
close to another human being. And he was *sooo* sweet,

always bringing Chinese food or pizza so I wouldn't have to cook.''

Rob said, ''You could be the person we've been looking for. We haven't really talked to anyone else he confided in.''

''Confided?''

''He seems to have been rather distant with most people.''

''Well, I wouldn't say he exactly confided in me. It wasn't like that. We were just . . . soul mates is the only way I can describe it. We knew everything we needed to know about each other without words. Does that make any sense?''

''Of course.''

Rob looked at me like I'd betrayed him, but I wasn't lying—I had once been fourteen.

''What finally happened?'' I said. ''Why did you stop seeing him?''

Again, tears welled. This time they spilled. ''Because I blew it, that's why. Everything was going along great, but I was stupid enough to tell him I loved him. I mean, isn't that the way it's supposed to be? If you love somebody, don't you say so? Isn't it nicer that way? But he said he wasn't ready for that. Well, naturally, I said that was fine, he could just go at whatever pace he needed to—I wouldn't say it again until he was ready to hear it. Because I knew he loved me. Nobody could treat me the way he did and not love me—he was the nicest guy I've ever met in my life. I mean, by far. They just don't make them like that anymore.

''But anyway, he just wasn't ready to make a commitment. So when I called him to find out why he hadn't called, he said he thought it was just best that we stop seeing each other for a while.'' She shrugged. ''And that was fine with me. I knew he'd come back.''

"And did he?"

I could have killed Rob—it opened the floodgates. She managed to stammer something that sounded like, "He never had a chance!" and then it was nonstop bawling for twenty minutes, with me trying to decide whether to pat her or not pat her, Rob trying to find tissues somewhere in her tiny studio, and Sarah coming thoroughly unglued.

Finally, when the attack began to subside, Rob cleared his throat. "I'm sorry this is so hard for you, Ms. Byers. But I know that you of all people want to make sure Jason's . . ." Rob couldn't bring himself to say "murderer," and I didn't blame him. Talking to Sarah Byers was really no different from talking to a child. He finally said, "I mean, I know you want to help us. What we were wondering is whether Jason ever talked to you about any enemies he might have had— anybody who had it in for him, wanted to do him harm."

"No way! Didn't you see the crowd at his wake? That man was universally loved. There wasn't a person in the whole city who didn't absolutely worship him."

"Somebody killed him."

"A crazy person, probably. I'm sure it'll turn out to be someone who never knew Jason at all."

I don't think I ever in my life saw a man gulp fresh air like Rob did when we were out of there. He staggered to the car, a broken man. "Rebecca, let's get a drink."

"You're supposed to be a hard-boiled reporter."

"I'm a wreck. Next time let's go watch a baby having open heart surgery or something. Something I can handle."

I had to admit it had been pretty harrowing. We drove back to the *Chronicle*, where Rob had left his car, and headed for the M&M, where generations of similarly wrecked reporters had drowned their sorrows. "One thing," he said, beer safely in hand and about three-quarters down the hatch, "a pattern seems to be emerging."

"You mean about Jason's women?"

"Yes. A first string and a second string, but he only slept with the second string."

"I thought a pattern was supposed to make sense."

CHAPTER 13

Carolyn Perlmutter consulted her notes. "It says here you think you have a lump in your breast."

"Carolyn. I do have a lump in my breast. I've felt it about eight times."

"Well, let's have a look."

As I lay back with my hands behind my head, the prescribed posture for breast examinations, I was aware of how wet my palms were. Fresh sweat was breaking out in my armpits. Every time fingers touched skin, I flinched.

"Nervous, huh?"

I'd been going to Carolyn for ten years. What did I have to hide? "Scared shitless."

She stopped, pawing over an area—the one where The Thing was—a little more thoroughly; then she did it again. Without saying anything, she went on to the other breast. She wasn't going to say a word until she'd finished the exam. But I couldn't stand it. "What do you think?"

"I feel something, but it's fibrous. I want to see if I can get fluid out of it."

"What's that about?"

"If I get fluid, we don't have to worry."

I watched her attach a needle to its syringe. At least it was a small one.

"Okay, try to relax."

Sure.

"Ouch."

"Okay. Let's wait a minute while that gets numb."

"That wasn't it?"

"That was the xylocaine." Now she attached a businesslike needle. I averted my eyes.

A moment later Carolyn was saying, "You can sit up now," by which I imagined the worst was over.

I rose, pulling up the hospital gown. She said, "I'd like to refer you to Charlie Suzawa. He's an excellent surgeon; really a prince of a guy, I promise you. Honestly, I refer everyone to him now."

I couldn't believe what she was saying. Hadn't she left out a chapter or three? "You didn't get any fluid?"

"No, I didn't. And with a lump as big as this one, I really think we need a surgeon's opinion."

"Oh, *opinion*. I thought I was going under the knife."

"He might—well, he'll probably want a biopsy."

A biopsy. There it was, the B word. I'd been expecting this; I had known I'd get sent for a biopsy. Why was the word so awful? Why was my heart pounding so hard? Because I was flat-out terrified, that was why. All it took was that one little word to reduce a competent lawyer to boneless protoplasm, a quivering puddle in the corner.

I got in my car and found my hands were shaking. Okay. I wouldn't drive drunk, and I shouldn't drive boneless. I got out and walked around the block, trying to breathe deeply, to banish the thing at least long enough to restore muscle coordination. But there is something about a purely physical fear without adrenaline behind it—it doesn't seem to respond to ordinary attempts to get rid of it. I finally got in and drove, the steering wheel so slick from sweat I knew I was dead if I had to react suddenly. Slow and easy, I thought; it's just a few blocks. Some creep on my rear end leaned on his horn, and the fear doubled. The car swerved nearly out of control, but I got it back in its lane. The creep passed on the right. If I'd had a coronary, my estate could have sued big.

It was too much to handle by myself. I sailed past Kruzick and right into Chris's office, where I plopped down in the client's chair. Chris looked up, alarmed. "What is it? You feel awful, don't you? Omigod, you're white as a ghost—which never look white to me, by the way. You must be alive."

"You see ghosts too?"

"I guess so, if you want to call them that. But not so much anymore—mostly whan I was a kid. And never, never anybody I knew or ever even heard of, just sort of nonpeople in period clothes."

"God, I'm glad it's you and not me!" That sounded so unpleasant I forgot my troubles for a second.

"So what's wrong? Have you got the flu? Jeez, I wonder if I can handle this by myself."

"I've got a lump in my breast. I have to have a biopsy."

"Ohhh." It was almost a moan, and instantly I felt better. It's too much, trying to handle a thing that big by yourself. "My poor peachblossom." But only for a second did I get to see the distress in her blue eyes. She closed them and withdrew, almost physically, like a turtle going into a shell. "It's okay," she said. "Thank God, it's okay."

"What are you talking about?"

"It's not cancer—or if it is, it's not life-threatening. Usually I don't do that, you know. Health things are too important. And also, I wouldn't read for you—I know you much too well.''

"I don't understand."

"The reading can be tainted by my own desires, my wishes for you. But sometimes I can get a hit—just one—without grounding or anything. I can just sort of tune in and there it is.''

"Grounding?''

"It means . . . I don't know, focusing is probably the best way to put it. You'll see us do it at the Raiders meeting.''

"What did you see then? What was it?''

"I took a look at both breasts, and I saw the lump—it's in the right one, isn't it?''

I nodded.

"It just looked constricted. I guess that's about the best way I can describe it.''

"I don't get it.''

"Well, I can't describe it. That's the best I can do.''

"How can you tell it's not serious?''

She shrugged. "I just asked if it's anything we have to worry about, and I got a no.''

I was starting to feel better. "Do you guarantee your work?''

"I wish.''

Kruzick walked in. "Rob for you, Rebecca.''

"Tell him—''

"He says it's important.''

I sighed and went to my office. I felt a little drained, but at least my palms were no longer flowing like the Nile. I was out of sorts, not much in a mood to deal with anything that wasn't life or death. "What's up?'' I more or less snapped.

"Adrienne didn't show up for work, and she didn't call in.''

I looked at my watch. It was ten-thirty. If she'd had to walk to work, she should have been there by now. "What do you think's happened?"

"I called her dad's, and he said she wasn't there—that she didn't stay there last night. I asked him where she did stay, and he said he didn't know."

"Fishy."

"Uh-huh. He says he doesn't know her friend Danno, which was the only other idea I had. I'm pretty worried, to tell you the truth."

"Have you called Curry and Martinez?"

"Oh sure. Right after I called the *Examiner*."

I closed my eyes and spoke to the darkness: "Should we be worried?"

It didn't answer.

"Rebecca? Are you there?"

"Listen, let's go knock on her door. I'd feel better."

"So would I."

Adrienne didn't answer. We looked at each other, shrugged, and started around the building, searching for open windows. There weren't any, but one window had a crack in it, more or less inviting us to take advantage of its weakness. "There couldn't be an alarm," said Rob. "It's not that kind of building."

"But there are laws."

"Something tells me we should go in."

"You and Chris."

"Huh?"

"Nothing. Look, maybe we should call the manager or something."

"Let's just test the window." He stood on a couple of concrete blocks and leaned against it. It gave and he shrugged. "Meant to be."

He climbed in. "I'll let you in the front door."

But I wasn't waiting. I clambered ungracefully over the sill, shredding my pantyhose in the process. The place smelled awful, mildew mixed with stale sweat. We were in the bedroom, which was dusty and apparently hadn't been touched. We wandered down the hall, peering in rooms, and near the living room I thought I heard something. What, I couldn't identify.

It must have been some slight movement, or perhaps nothing at all, just the awareness of another human being. She was there, mouth open, sheet pulled up to her neck.

"Adrienne?" Why hadn't she heard us break the window? "Adrienne!"

"She's dead," said Rob.

But I touched her; she was warm. I felt for a pulse and got one, but it seemed very faint. "I'm no nurse, but I think she's in a coma. Let's look in the bathroom."

My hunch had been right—empty pill bottles were everywhere. One glance convinced us she'd taken everything in sight. We dialed 911, and I rode with her to the hospital, the empty bottles in a plastic bag in my purse. Rob followed in his car. On the way, I talked to her, the way you're supposed to talk to a person in a coma, begging her to hang on, telling her we all loved her, hoping it sounded okay even if I'd just met her. The truth was that as little as I knew her, I desperately wanted her to live, and thought this must be the way people feel who work in emergency rooms. We all feel, I guess, that life is so fragile we're frantic to hang on to it, even if it's someone else's.

Rob phoned her father, and the two of us waited for him while they pumped her stomach, holding hands as if we were still lovers, and once again my palms could have watered a geranium.

For once, Rob seemed unable to talk. He looked around and said, "It's all so . . . stark." And then he shut up.

Like your life, I thought. *Empty. Sad.*

I don't know why I thought that—it just came to me, like one of Chris's psychic messages. Rob didn't seem a sad person; he was constantly in motion. But you never got below the surface with him, and it made you wonder if there was anything down there to find. Maybe he really was a human news-gathering machine.

An intern came out. "Are you here for Adrienne Dunson?"

"Yes, but we're not relatives. We're just the ones who found her."

"She's being moved to intensive care."

"Will she make it?"

He shrugged. "She's pretty bad."

I left to call Dr. Suzawa, who'd just had a cancellation and could see me that afternoon at three. When I got back, Rob was talking to Adrienne's dad. Not wanting to make his reacquaintance, I hung back, thinking about the coming ordeal.

On the way back to the office, I turned it over and over in my mind—the impulse I had to ask Rob to go with me. Why was it so strong? I wondered.

And decided it was partly because I was so frightened. And also because we'd been close once. But probably most of all because a part of me still loved him and wanted him back, just like it used to be. But it wasn't fair to call on him now, to ask him for help as if we were still together. Perhaps Chris would go with me.

But she wasn't in the office, having left to continue

reading the seemingly endless output of Jason Mc-Kendrick. I ended up going alone, but it turned out fine. Carolyn had apparently called to pave the way.

Suzawa greeted me with a rueful smile. "Dr. Perlmutter tells me you hate the kind of doctor who has you into the office to describe the procedure, has you back for the procedure, and, as she says you put it, makes you come back a third time to get the results." He paused. "Of course, most of us feel it's best for the patient that way."

"It's best for your own bank accounts," I snapped, coming out with something I'd normally be way too wimpy to say. I heard someone say once that anger covers fear and fear covers anger. Meaning I might be talking tough, but underneath I was scared to death.

Unexpectedly, Suzawa laughed. "Well, some people just aren't ready the first time. But since Carolyn called, I made sure I have time to do the procedure today. And you can phone for the results, but I'm afraid you do have to come back. I'll need to check on the wound to make sure it's healing properly."

"That seems okay," I said, not wanting to give in but unable to refute the logic of it. I'd had a doctor tell me once I had to come back because otherwise there was a likelihood of "misunderstanding." Like the audio quality was better in his office. And when I got there, sure enough, he mentioned my test was normal and I should go and sin no more. The insurance company lost eighty bucks on the deal, and I've been stewing about it ever since.

"Shall we do it?" said Suzawa, "or would you like to watch the video first?"

I loathe the videos specialists show you. "Why don't you sum it up?" I said.

"Basically, it says there are several methods of

screening for cancer. You've already had cyst aspiration, which didn't tell us much, and I'm afraid none of the others would either, if the lump is benign. Some are useful if the result is positive, but if it's negative, we still can't rule out cancer. Do you follow?''

"Perfectly."

"In other words, what we call an open surgical biopsy, as opposed to a core needle biopsy, is what I'd recommend for you."

I liked his straightforward approach and obvious willingness to accommodate me; and I adored not having to watch the video. I was convinced; there was no alternative but to have the biopsy. "Let's do it," I said.

"That's all the questions you have? Carolyn said you were tough."

"I haven't been tough enough?" I thought I'd been downright obstreperous. "Okay, what are the consequences?"

"Well, you will have a scar. And there'll be bruising and maybe some drainage into the bandage."

"I can handle it." Any of that was better than the fear.

The thing itself was nothing, really, not much more than the aspiration. He and his nurse, in surgical greens, painted my breast with iodine, draped it in sterile towels, and then numbed it with novocaine. After that, he made an incision and spread the breast open with what he said were retractors—things that looked like bent forks—and about then I quit watching. I did notice he came for the lump with scissors, which didn't look too terrifying, and after that, it was only a matter of sewing me up.

No big deal. The hard part would be the waiting.

CHAPTER 14

I knew I wasn't going to be walking into a pack of gypsies with head scarves and crystal balls, but the Raiders of the Lost Art were still a pretty daunting bunch. Chris had told me to come to Rosalie's a little late, that they had some business to do before I got there. She's never answered my veiled queries on the subject, but I think they wanted to take a psychic peek at the visitor before she arrived in full legal eagledom.

I think I passed. At any rate, Tanesha apologized for being so inhospitable at her office, and I said I was sorry I'd shown up without calling. Ivan said he hoped he hadn't terrified me with his offers to lay on hands, but he couldn't help it, he really thought he could help me. Moonblood seemed guarded as ever, and Rosalie was herself—a pretty comfortable and pretty smart person, maternal with an overlay of something that might once have been called wisdom. She was the sort of woman who in tribal times would have been a shaman, I imagined, respected by everyone for her insight and her wisdom. Here, she lived in poverty and more or less disrepute on the edge of the Western Addition. The irony of it suddenly came clear to me: what passes for a shaman these days is ridiculed as hopelessly New Age.

I don't know, maybe all that's an exaggeration based on my reaction to her. What I can say objectively is that

I was very glad to see her again, that I was drawn to
her in the same way I had once been drawn to my kin-
dergarten teacher, Mrs. Rooney, fixer of skinned knees
and dispenser of hugs.

Rosalie offered tea, which I accepted, very excellent
Japanese tea, and said they were pleased to have me
there. I thought Moonblood grimaced, but I couldn't be
sure. "We thought you might like a little warm-up,"
she said. "What do you know about what we do?"

I thought about it. What had Chris really told me?
"Almost nothing," I said.

"Would you like us to do a little reading for you
before we tackle Chris's problem?"

"Sure."

"Okay. What you'll basically see is a group of people
closing their eyes—because it's easier to focus that
way—for a few minutes before talking. But what we're
doing behind the eyelids is going to vary. I picked this
group for its different talents. Ivan, as you might imagine, is clairsentient."

"I beg your pardon?"

"I get feelings in the body," said Ivan. "That's how
I take in information. Like, for instance, I'm really good
on people's new sweeties."

"Yeah, just not your own," said Tanesha. "I think
we read about that Janice Applewhite nine times probably before she finally disappeared with your CD player
and your favorite cat."

"The cat was a blow, goddammit. Why'd she have to
take my cat?"

"Well, I'll tell you one damn thing. If you find that
cat, it's gonna have to be by hiring a detective. I'm not
reading about Janice and Babycakes one more time.
That girl was a junkie opportunist; you could see it
miles away."

"She was not a junkie!"

"What do you mean she wasn't a junkie? The girl took your CD player, your cat, every pill in your medicine cabinet, and every drop in your liquor cabinet. Just because you didn't happen to have any heroin on hand doesn't mean she wasn't a junkie."

"Well, look, did I call it about that Tyson Cooper you almost got involved with?"

"Well, that's different. That wasn't about you."

"That's what I *mean*. I can do it as long as it's somebody else." He turned to me. "See, I take in information through the body."

"I beg your pardon?"

"Through the solar plexus, or the hara. Not through the head, like most people. I get feelings. You know?"

"Like whether it's going to rain?"

He shrugged, and there was an uncomfortable silence. I was on the verge of apologizing when Moonblood said, "Look, it's hard enough to talk about this stuff without a bunch of cheap shots."

It had been a cheap shot, and I was sorry. On the other hand, surely it was just as hard to understand as it was to talk about. No, I didn't know what Ivan meant, and yet to say so, I was sure, was just going to elicit a smugness ("Ha, ha, I know and you don't") that I'd already seen snatches of.

Rosalie stepped in quickly. "Moonblood," said Rosalie, "is a true specialist. She can do what's called psychometry. In fact, we're going to try it when the police give back Chris's car. She can probably sit in it and pick up something."

"But what?"

Moonblood spoke. "Well, I think if I had something belonging to a suspect, I could tell if he'd been there or not."

''Then there's Tanesha,'' said Rosalie.

Tanesha said, ''I hear voices,'' and hummed the ''Twilight Zone'' theme. ''That's the one they put you away for. So s'cuse *me* if I'm a little nervous at the office.''

''It's called clairaudient,'' said Rosalie.

''You know what I've always wondered? Are they outside your head or inside?''

''Inside. You know how you have a mental TV screen? Well, I've got a radio in there.''

I guessed I did, too. I heard voices all the time: Rebecca, could you try a little harder, please? Would you mind getting it right this time? That sort of thing. Or little warnings in court sometimes: Don't ask him that. It's going to start something you don't want to start.

I'd learned to heed them. But it was hard to imagine that David Berkowitz, Tanesha, and I were all clairaudients.

''I guess the difference in me and crazy people,'' Tanesha said, ''is I only get them when I ask something. I mean, the information just comes in words instead of pictures.''

''Chris and I are clairvoyants,'' Rosalie said. ''Although I guess all of us do a little bit of everything. You can't predict how the information is going to come. And of course most of us see energy to some extent. That can also take a lot of forms. And it can look different at different times. Once a client came in and he had a great big red circle around him. Now I don't see that every day—just then.''

''What did it mean?''

''That was a seriously angry man. He was getting divorced, and it got ugly.''

''That was the sort of thing that made me think I was going crazy,'' said Chris. ''These wild things that seemed to come out of nowhere.''

"Some of them," I said, "in costume, right?"

She flushed. "Listen, Rebecca. If we ever split up the partnership, don't tell anyone I see ghosts, okay?"

It was a joke, but it brought home once again how much it had cost her to let me in on her secret.

"Before we do your reading," Chris said, "I have to ask Rosalie something."

She whispered; Rosalie shook her head; they negotiated; and finally Rosalie nodded. She said, "Chris wants me to do my parlor trick. I hate doing it because it's sort of showoffy, but she talked me into it."

"Yaaay," said Ivan.

Tanesha said, "You're not going to believe what this woman can do."

Rosalie rummaged, finally found a pad and an envelope. "Here's what you do. Write me a question on this pad, fold the paper up, and seal it in the envelope. And make it a different question from the one you're going to ask us all to read about."

"Why? What's going to happen?"

"I'll answer the question without reading it."

Okay, fine. If she could do a trick, so could I. I wrote, folded, and sealed.

Rosalie took the envelope, closed her eyes, and turned the envelope over. She rubbed it some. At no time did she open her eyes or even lower her chin. When she finally opened her eyes, she handed me the envelope. Her face was full of compassion, as if she could hardly bear to deliver the bad news.

"My dear," she said, "I'm afraid I can't offer you a lot of hope. Honestly, I don't see a future for this project. Now, things could change. I don't know how hard you're working on it now, or how far along it is, but I get the feeling, I really feel strongly, that nothing will change until you put a lot more energy behind it. I know it's hard, trying to do two things at once, but I just don't think this is going to fly until you're able to devote a lot more time to it. Does that make any sense?''

I nodded. ''Thank you,'' I said, and felt very ashamed of myself.

Chris said, ''Well? She got it, didn't she? Will you tell what the question was?''

''Rosalie, you tell them.''

''Rebecca wanted to know when her book would be published.''

I gasped. Her answer had been good, in fact perfect, but I'd had no idea she'd know *exactly* what the question was.

''You aren't writing a book!'' Chris said.

''Well, it was a parlor trick, so I asked a trick question. I figured if Rosalie was any good, she'd know it was a trick.''

''It doesn't work like that,'' said Rosalie. ''A big part of this is knowing what questions to ask. If I'd thought to ask if you were sincere, I might have found out there was no book, and then I'd have *really* looked clever. Instead, I took the question literally.''

I thought about her answer. ''Well, there's certainly nothing wrong with your information source. But how did you know the question?''

She turned her palms up. ''I went to see another psychic who does this same thing, out of a garage down the peninsula. Couldn't believe it, but couldn't resist trying. What do you know, it worked. I haven't got a clue how I do it. But I do have to hold the paper; that much I figured out. Now Ivan's clairsentient, so you'd think he'd be the one, but he only gets it if it's a relationship question. You'd think health would be his specialty, but Moonblood's better on that. Your partner, by the way, is a genius on fire.''

"Fire? Why didn't you tell us about the Oakland Hills?'' Hundreds of homes there had been destroyed by fire the year before.

"Nobody asked me,'' said Chris. "But remember that time I told you your transmission sounded funny and you'd better have it checked?''

"I was impressed that you knew what a transmission sounded like. But it wasn't that, by the way. It was something to do with the gas line and the manifold.''

"I don't even know what a horn sounds like. I just knew something in there was about to go up in flames.''

"Oh.'' This was a little like having a guardian angel.

"Well, look, let's do your reading. You get to ask us a question, and we'll all work on it.''

Rosalie said, "Okay, we're going to ground. That means we'll get ourselves in a receptive state, like a focus. In fact, why don't I start it, and then everybody can finish their own way.''

"Wait. How do you know when you're ready to read?''

Chris said, "I get a little body sensation.''

"A twitch or a tickle or what?''

"Well, it's like—'' She stopped, looked puzzled. "Maybe it isn't a body sensation. It's kind of a 'ping', only it isn't a sound.''

"That certainly clears things up,'' said Tanesha. She looked at me. "Look, you just know, okay?''

"Let's go,'' said Rosalie, and they all closed their eyes. "Imagine you have a red cord running down your spine, all the way, till it comes out your body. Drop it now, drop it into the Earth; drop it through the floor, through the neighbor's apartment, through all seven floors to the basement. Drop it through the basement, into the soft Earth. Go down gradually, ever gradually through the layers; go through the roots you find there, down, down, until you hit bedrock, and go through the bedrock, down, down, until it starts to get warm. Go farther, till you get to the Earth's core, its molten white-hot core, and start to draw some of the Earth's energy up through your cord.''

She went on another few minutes, during which the Raiders were instructed to raise the Earth's energy into their bodies and then return it to the Earth on the left side of the cord, so that a continual circuit was formed. I didn't get it, but it certainly wasn't spooky, and I did see how it could focus your mind. Gradually, each person's eyes popped open. Ivan asked for something of mine to hold, and I gave him my watch.

Rosalie said, ''Everybody ready?''

Nods all around.

''What's the question?''

I thought a minute. I could have asked about The Thing, but I was going to know the answer soon enough anyway. I said, ''What should I do about my relationship with my boyfriend?''

''Julio?'' said Chris.

I stared at her.

She shrugged. ''Well, you've been spending a lot of time with Rob lately. Also, you're into trick questions.''

''Julio.''

They closed their eyes again.

Chris opened hers first. ''Marry him,'' she said.

''What?''

''Just kidding. I don't think I can do this because I know you so well and I'm crazy about Julio. I did get that, but I think it was simple envy talking.''

Ivan said, "I'm getting a pun, I think. Is there anything we should know about Julio involving water?"

"Well, he's a marine biologist."

"Damn! That's it. Okay, so the relationship is not necessarily 'all wet,' huh?"

"I don't know. It could be. We seem to have some insurmountable problems."

Rosalie said, "Let me take a shot. Rebecca, I know it seems like the problems are insurmountable, but I'm not sure that's the case. I think you've been hurt by someone else, maybe you feel more or less betrayed, and Julio is a very warm person; a very giving person; and you love him for that. You need that. But right now I think you don't realize how afraid you are that the same thing might happen with him that happened before. So you're reluctant to get too involved and therefore the problems seem bigger than they really are. The thing is, the relationship is great for Julio for the same reason.

"I like this guy. He's a truly generous-hearted man. But he's in the same place you are. Something bad happened to him—is he divorced?"

"Yes."

"That's it then. He hasn't really gotten over the divorce." She put up a hand. "Not the marriage. He's over the marriage, he doesn't want the ex-wife back, he just doesn't want to make himself that vulnerable again. Yet. Now things could definitely change, just like with that book of yours, but he's enjoying being with you partly because he thinks the problems are insurmountable, therefore he doesn't have to make up his mind to be vulnerable again. Does that make any sense?"

My stomach had done something, but I wasn't sure what. Maybe it was one of those physical sensations Chris mentioned that aren't really physical. Kind of a ping that wasn't. It was something I got sometimes with certain clients I didn't really trust. I got it when they were telling the truth.

I nodded, unable to speak.

"Tanesha?"

"I like this guy. You did all right for yourself, Miss Becky." I flinched—no one calls me Becky. "This is one fine dude. I get the feeling that down the line you two might work something out, but I don't think the time's right for now. Has marriage been mentioned?"

"No. Nothing like that." Not even living together.

"You come from a family that expects a lot of you, don't you?"

I'd never thought of it like that, but I supposed it was true.

"See, they expect a lot from you so you expect a lot of yourself. I get the feeling you think you've got to know where you're going, with everything you do. You've got to have goals. Well, maybe you don't right now. Maybe the best thing you could do in this situation is just relax and enjoy it. I hate to be the bearer of bad news, but that's how I see it."

Moonblood said, "Yeah, I haven't got anything to add. The guy's good stuff, I guess we all agree on that. But I'm getting something weird, and the more I try to figure it out, the less sense it makes. So I'll just tell you and see if it means anything. It's the moon. Not a full moon, and not a crescent—sort of a half moon I guess you'd say."

"I—uh—no, I guess I can't figure it out." Secretly, I thought it had something to do with her name. "Do you get moons a lot?"

"No, but I do get these real practical kinds of things. Really, really straightforward. That's kind of my thing."

I shrugged. For the life of me, I couldn't make it mean anything.

Ivan said, "There's another person here. Didn't anyone see another person?"

My heart fluttered.

"Don't worry, it's not a rival. Nothing like that. Just someone Julio's worried about; and you're worried too. But you're not worried about the person, you're worried about yourself, how you'll be with him or her, I can't tell which it is. Wait a minute! It's a kid, isn't it? Does Julio have a kid?"

"Esperanza."

He nodded. "I see her now. He doesn't want her to get hurt. He's afraid if you two get any closer and you dump him, the kid'll be hurt. And you're not sure you're ready to be a mother. Is that it?"

I wasn't ready to be a mother? I hadn't even thought about that aspect of it. Would I be Esperanza's mother? A lot of the time I would. A scary thought.

I saw what Ivan meant.

"Listen to the man," said Tanesha. "Relationships are his thing."

They haven't told me anything I didn't know, I thought. But I had to admit they'd given me some new ways of thinking about things. I liked the relax-and-enjoy-it theory.

"Come on, let's do Chris," said Moonblood.

Chris said, "Yes. Now or never."

"What's the question?"

"Let's do two. First, let's just look at some names and see if we can get anything on whether they killed Jason. Then let's do, 'How can I get out of this mess?' "

"Are you going to read?" I was puzzled.

"I can look at the names, but I don't really trust myself. Everybody ready? Adrienne, Tommy, Vanda."

"Just first names? Why is that?"

"Who knows? But usually it's all you need."

Moonblood said, "Adrienne's turning black on me. Is she black?"

"No."

"Well, something's wrong. She's not well."

"She tried to kill herself today."

Moonblood and Ivan nodded. Ivan said, "I can't tell if she killed him, though. Just that she feels really bad about it. Almost like she's guilty, but when I ask the question she doesn't light up."

"How about Tommy?"

"Shit, girl, good thing this one's not your partner's boyfriend. Know how I get those stupid songs sometimes? I get 'Mack the Knife' on Mr. Tommy. This dude is nobody to mess around with. I don't see him in that car, though. On the other hand, I wouldn't want to be in the same room with him and a sharp object."

"Anybody else?"

Rosalie said, "I don't think it's any of them."

"Okay, Felicity."

They got nothing on her either. Ivan said, "Come on, this is Mickey Mouse. Let's do the other question."

"Okay. What can I do to get out of this?"

This time they sat with their eyes closed a long time, nearly five minutes, I thought.

Finally, Tanesha opened hers and said, "It's funny, but I don't think you're in any danger except from the cops. I don't see any enemies. But how can that be?"

Moonblood said, "I'm getting one of my weird advice things. Go home and look in your kitchen. Does that mean anything?"

"Dirty dishes."

"Could 'kitchen' be a metaphor?" I asked.

"Let's see. A place where there's food. A restaurant.

A sort of back room in a house—maybe in the head? Something on a back burner?''

Moonblood shook her head. ''My stuff is much too literal. If I got kitchen, it probably meant that. So do me a favor—go home and look in your kitchen, okay?''

Chris smiled. ''I'm so depressed I was going to have some ice cream anyway.''

Rosalie said, ''Chris, I get the feeling the answer is connected with something in the past.''

I was disappointed. How smart did you have to be to figure that out?

Chris said, ''You mean like a fight with someone? Something like that?''

''I don't think so.'' She closed her eyes again. ''It's not the distant past, either, but it's long past in your mind.''

Ivan nodded. ''I'm getting, like a floor under a bed with dust mice all over it. And maybe one old shoe.''

''Like I swept it under the rug?''

''More like you just forgot about it.''

''Oh, great. So my right course of action is remember it.''

Everyone looked downcast.

''You mean that's *all*?''

We were quiet. Disappointment filled the room like the buzzing of a fly. Finally, Rosalie spoke, looking at me. ''This stuff is bits and pieces, like mosaic tiles. If we could get a whole picture . . .''

''. . . we could win the lottery,'' Ivan and Moonblood said together. I gathered Rosalie had mentioned this notion before.

''I just want to say one other thing,'' Tanesha said. ''I asked if you needed to look out for danger. And I got that whoever set you up wasn't really malicious.''

''They murdered somebody!''

"I mean toward you. You know . . . at least you don't have to worry about anything from that quarter."

On the way home, Chris grumbled mightily. "Some friend, right? They just happened to set me up because—what?—I was handy? Well, isn't that just great—no enemy."

"You always said you didn't have one."

"Now I wish I did."

There's no pleasing some people. As for me, I thought I got a great reading. It had definitely made a believer out of me, especially that funny thing Moon-blood said, once I figured it out. Julio and I had joked about moving to some midpoint between our two towns. Half Moon Bay would be just about right.

CHAPTER 15

Rob was in my office when I arrived the next morning. "I've been doing a little spadework."

"Want some coffee?"

"Yeah. Now listen—"

"Caffeine first, okay?"

Kruzick loved nothing better than serving coffee to clients. It was all we could do to keep him from wearing a little French maid's uniform with biscuit hat for the task. And half the time, despite our best efforts, he affected a falsetto accent while pouring anyway. All very amusing, *une petite* role reversal, *très charmante*. Except that he made inhumanly egregious coffee. We'd tried everything, including watching him through each step, and he got no better. We went through about ten kinds of coffee-makers till we finally found one that, for some reason, seemed to click with him. Now his coffee was close to drinkable. He insisted on pouring it into a china pot and serving it in thin cups with saucers.

This morning, in answer to my request, he arrived tray in hand, carefully lined with a starched white napkin, and he wore an embroidered apron. *"Café pour m'sieu et mam'selle? Madeleine?"* He had a plate of cookies on the tray.

"Alan, I appreciate the service, but the bunny dip really isn't necessary."

159

"Oh, pas probleme, mam'selle. Nous aimons a plaisir."

See what I have to put up with? Why can't Mickey go out with a nice doctor?

When the drug had started to work (about the third sip), Rob blurted his news: "I found out Adrienne's mother committed suicide about six months ago."

"That poor girl must have been through hell. No wonder she's so depressed." I paused and thought about it. "What do we know about the suicide? Had she been ill?"

"I can't find out anything. Adrienne's dad clams up on the subject. I talked to him this morning." He stopped and sipped for a minute. "Well, I might as well tell you the whole thing. I found out about the mom from the famous Danno—you know the ex-boyfriend she keeps talking about? She'd called him a few times, and he finally called her back. But he got nervous because he couldn't reach her either at Jason's or her dad's, so he called the *Chronicle* and finally the call got to me. Anyway, he let it slip about the mom, but he didn't know the details; so I went over to the hospital and found Mr. Dunson there—what's his name?—Fred, I think. He wouldn't talk to me."

"What do you mean wouldn't talk to you? He said 'no comment' or flipped you off, or what?"

"I mean, he just sat in a corner with his head down and wouldn't acknowledge I was there. Finally, I got worried, thinking, what with his wife dying and now his daughter in intensive care, maybe he'd gone off the deep end or something. So I started saying was he okay, and he really had to buck up—don't throw up now. . . ."

"No, I think that's nice."

". . . and he went ballistic on me. Started yelling it

was none of my business and to butt out of his life. As you can imagine, all hell broke loose in the hospital. White-coated people came from miles around, and he got this look, like a cornered fox—I don't blame him, it must have been terrifying. Maybe he thought they were going to lock him up or something, I don't know, but it was abundantly obvious he felt the time had come to leave, and he wasn't sure they were going to let him. So he knocked me down to clear a path.''

"Knocked you down?" My voice was a little weird, but I thought I was going to be all right.

"Yeah, he just came out and hit me. . . . Hey, what's wrong?''

Rob had been so engrossed in his story, which I think he more or less perceived as funny, that he hadn't noticed the lower half of my face trembling or my funny voice. By now I'd teared up, and great, embarrassing trails of saltwater were making their way down my face.

"Look, I'm okay—it didn't hurt a bit, honest." He paused, trying to figure me out. "Rebecca? Hey, I didn't know you cared.''

"It's not you. It's just so sad—first the mom and now maybe the daughter. And that poor man half out of his mind about the whole thing.''

"Yeah, well, he drinks, too.''

But I was sunk in the Dunson family drama, and sobbing.

"Hey. Hey, hold on a minute." He looked nearly as confused as when Adrienne had cried and needed him to hold her. But he had the sense to gather me up without being prodded. "It's okay. That's a good girl. Cry all you want. That's a baby." If I weren't in such a state I would have fallen off my chair at the realization he even knew these phrases. Perhaps he'd been dating a mother with a baby.

Finally, when I was starting to get a grip, he pushed me away, as he had Adrienne, and looked me straight in the eye, assessing. "Something's wrong. Something's really wrong. This isn't like you. You're raw. That's why that story got you, because your hide's thin."

Hide was a good word in the circumstances, one Dr. Freud would have approved of; that was what I couldn't do anymore.

I tried to muster bravado. "I'm scared, that's all." I spoke as if it were nothing. "I had a breast biopsy yesterday."

His face was a picture of confidence shattered: one minute I was strong, healthy Rebecca, the next I was a broken victim. His voice was a croak: "You have . . ." long pause ". . . cancer?"

"The test results aren't in. But I've got a lump, and I'm scared. I'm a little weird." I said again, "That's all," and wondered if that would satisfy him, if he would change the subject.

He said, "Why didn't you tell me?" nearly whispering, incredulous.

"I just felt like it was more than anyone could deal with right now. Chris's career depends on my being strong. I didn't want to be a liability." He looked utterly unbelieving. "I don't know! I just couldn't talk about it. It was too close to the bone to hand over to another human being—and it was killing me not to do that. You see how I am. It was nuts." I let that stand for a second and then I blurted, "Don't you have any secrets?"

He just stared, alarm in every cell, every bit the trapped fox Dunson had been. I didn't let him off the hook.

I said, "Come on, you know mine. Don't you have one?"

In a moment he recovered enough to say, "You don't have to change the subject. You can talk about it."

But I was thinking about that look, the trapped-fox look, and what it meant. He'd never told me he loved me, I thought, never told me good-bye when I broke away, never said he'd miss me. *Never anything*, I thought. *Does he have feelings? Are they his secrets?*

I thought I'd hit on something. I knew he had feelings, some of them for me—I could tell by the look on his face when I said the B word. But never, never was I going to hear it from Mr. Rob I'm-a-self-contained-unit Burns. The thought of it made me cry again. Through what was left of my formerly tough hide, just a veil of thin, thin skin, I seemed to be absorbing everyone's pain.

"Beck? Beck, what is it?" The silvery mane of my father—and the rest of his head—poked in the office.

"Daddy!"

"I—uh—I guess I should have called." He looked acutely embarrassed, and then angry. "Rob, what's going on here?" He spoke like some medieval king challenging a knight who'd made his daughter cry. The last thing I needed was time travel to the twelfth century.

"Dad, this is none of your business."

Like a dog paddled for something it doesn't understand, Rob stared at the floor. My hero. "Hello, Isaac."

My father gave him the glare that had been turning witnesses to jelly for nearly half a century. In a moment, Rob would confess on the stand: "I did it! I killed Rebecca with my little hatchet."

I wanted to yell at them both. I turned to get my coat and in the process heard Rob say, "I was just leaving."

I shrugged into the jacket, turning back to Dad, seeing Rob's back. He didn't even say, "See ya," having apparently forgotten my existence.

"Come on, Dad, let's take a walk. Suddenly I need a whole lot of air."

My father was nearly seventy. Was he too old a dog to learn anything? Probably, but I felt stepped on; surely feminism began at home.

I was so angry I didn't speak on the elevator ride, and only when I felt a blast of cold air (in San Francisco we have it even in August) did I speak. "You know what that felt like? Like not being in a room at all. You had no right to accuse Rob."

"I didn't accuse him."

"The hell you didn't! Your voice did, and the question did. Whatever was going on in there was between Rob and me, not Rob and you."

"You're my daughter."

"I'm an adult. Also, what was going on was not your business. But be that as it may, if you wanted to stick your nose in, I was the person to address, not the other person because he happened to be male."

"I was trying to protect you."

"My point exactly. I'm not two, Dad. I can protect myself."

"Well, it looked like you were doing a piss-poor job."

Dad, it had nothing to do with Rob. I was upset because I might have cancer.

I couldn't say that now. As inappropriate as it was for Dad to try to protect me from Rob, it would have been great to have some paternal comfort about The Thing. But I couldn't ask now. I'd gotten up this head of righteous indignation that said, Don't mess with me, I'm strong. I couldn't switch gears in mid-tantrum.

In the end, it was better, I guess. I had hated being treated like some teenage princess by my very politically correct father, but now that that was over, the anger it left in its wake felt a lot better than feeling sorry for myself.

We walked in silence for a while, me huffing with righteousness and Dad thinking it over, I guess. Finally, he said, "I'm sorry, Beck. I won't do it again." But his blue eyes twinkled. "Maybe."

"Okay." I put out my hand. "Truce."

He sighed. "I thought I'd finally passed Feminism 101."

"Just don't open any doors."

He laughed. Mickey objected to this, though I didn't. I said, "What made you drop by, anyway?"

"I wanted some of Alan's fabulous coffee."

"Bleeagh. Well, I'm glad to see you. I wouldn't mind getting your opinion on McKendrick and Chris."

It was probably what he'd come to talk about anyway. The story had been heavily covered by all the local media, but aside from a polite call the first day, both my parents had pretty well kept their noses out of it. Which was a great thing, especially in the case of Mom. But Dad was the best lawyer in town, and since I had access to a free opinion, I was going for it.

He said, "Are you sure she didn't do it?"

"What!" I couldn't believe my ears. Chris was family.

He patted the air, okay-okay. "Just checking. You'd have some intuitive feeling if something didn't ring right."

"Do you rely on intuition a lot?" I hadn't told him about Chris's little psychic problem.

He looked shocked. "All the time. Don't you?"

I pondered. "I don't know. I just don't know."

"I'll tell you what mine says now—or maybe it's just common sense."

"What?"

"Chris knows something."

It was all I could do not to say, 'How dare you question her? How could you?' Instead, I said, "She says she never even met McKendrick."

"Well, then, I'd believe her on that. But it wasn't coincidence her car was used. How could it have been? Someone had to follow her to that movie." (I'd made the Raiders meeting a movie so as to keep her secret, yet make clear she didn't have a decent alibi.)

"All she'll say is she doesn't have any enemies."

"Famous last words. Look, she probably knows something she doesn't know she knows. Could it be that?"

"I think it could. But what?"

"Maybe she should try hypnosis."

"It's a thought." A formidable thought. Here was someone who already spent lots of her time in a trance. If we could find a reputable hypnotist, it could be a great shortcut. I told Dad about Tommy La Barre.

He shook his head unhappily. "I don't know, Beck. You better hope it's not him. This is the kind of guy who's going to have an unshakeable alibi."

"If he hired someone, maybe they'll turn up."

"How? You think they'll find Jesus and suffer remorse?"

"I thought you might have some ideas."

"Thanks for the vote of confidence. When looking for a hit man, see Isaac Schwartz."

"Omigod, that's a great idea. I just meant I thought you might be able to think of a strategy. But come to think of it, you know half the unsavory characters in town."

"And those I don't know probably carry my tattered business card just in case. But La Barre's probably connected. I stay as far as possible from those people."

"Yes, but some of your ex-clients probably know people who know people. How about making some inquiries?"

"People get killed for that kind of inquiry."

"Come on, Dad. Nobody's going to kill Isaac Schwartz—who's going to be the killer's lawyer when his case comes to trial?"

"With all due modesty, you have a point. Okay, I'll phone around. But I just gave myself an idea with that remark about my esteemed clientele carrying my card. Maybe that's why McKendrick had Chris's number—because she'd been recommended as a lawyer."

"But why hasn't the person who recommended her come forward?"

"Well, that's easy. Because they don't know her car was used in the murder and couldn't possibly know her name and number was in his pocket."

"I don't know—I've talked to a lot of McKendrick's friends." But I knew it need not be a friend. It could be the most casual acquaintance. And the theory still didn't explain why her car was used—unless that person was the murderer.

Now that had merit. But still—why frame Chris?

I figured I must have formed something in the neighborhood of fifteen theories about the type of person who'd killed McKendrick and the circumstances under which it had happened, yet none of them covered everything. Everywhere I turned there was some dead end, some unexplained detail. It was the most frustrating thing I'd ever run into.

"Rebecca Schwartz. Roger DeCampo." The Cosmic Blind Date was standing right in my path, blocking my way, sounding like a prison guard and holding out his right hand to be shaken. In a daze I obliged and introduced Dad. "What are you doing in these parts?" I asked.

"You know that little problem I told you about? The one you're going to help on? I came down to do a little work on that."

"But, Roger, I thought we agreed I couldn't take the case."

"We didn't agree to anything. You said you wouldn't, that's all. But you will." He gave me one of those bottom-of-the-face smiles; frankly, I found it chilling.

"Nice to see you, Roger." I glanced at my watch. "I'm afraid we're late."

I pushed past him, Dad following a little reluctantly—he hated rudeness.

Roger shouted over his shoulder, "I'll call you."

"Former client?" Dad said.

"I'll tell you all about it. But first, what's your take on him?"

"He seemed to be having a little trouble with reality—saying you're going to take a case you've refused. And I didn't like the smile."

I wondered if Chris had been right about Roger all the time.

I told Dad the story. "What do you think?"

"Well, I guess he must be a little nuts. I mean, even if the subject weren't UFOs, how could a sane person get so involved with other people's obsessions?"

Suddenly I had a new thought. He'd said to me, "It may not be obvious to you, but I am one of the major players of the universe." I'd thought he was joking, what else was I to think? But maybe he was just a guy who wanted to belong, and the UFO club was what had invited him.

I thought about the human need to be special, how we all want to believe we're somebody just a little more

important than the next guy. What if you had nice
friends, perfectly ordinary, but also very special people
who told you you'd been seen at the Interplanetary
Council? I tried to imagine people saying it to me:
"Now, Rebecca, it's written in the Akashic Records.
You! Yes, you. Well, you'd better believe it because it's
true. You're really a very important person, galactically
speaking. Sure, the world's full of lawyers, but how
many of them are making the kinds of decisions that
influence the course of history?"

I'd at least be intrigued. And if they were people I
really trusted, really liked very much—Chris and Julio,
say—I might, in time, come to want very much to join
their club, in much the same way I'd suddenly em-
braced Chris's psychic world view. What a wonderful
escape it would be! I wouldn't be crazy, really. Just
someone who had crackpot ideas. But if I started to live
more and more in that world, I'd probably get weirder
and weirder, much as Roger seemed to be doing. It was
a little like a cult, I thought—sort of a pervasive self-
hypnosis.

Dad said, "Still, I knew a perfectly nice woman
who'd been abducted by spacemen. Someone I respected. I didn't know about the ETs until I'd known
her a few years—she got tipsy at a party and told me
about it."

"Do you think she was lying?"

"Actually, I'm inclined to believe it. She seemed
pretty damn sure."

"You believe in ETs?"

"Well, I didn't till then."

CHAPTER
16

Chris hadn't been in the office when I left, but she was very much there when I got back—and practically on fire: "I've got the missing piece."

I sank down in her clients' chair. "Well, for God's sake, what is it?"

"It's something in the past all right, just like Rosalie said. But it's so trivial, just so *tiny*, you'd never think of it. And you'd never in a million years connect it with some big drama in your life."

I was going to jump up and down and scream if she didn't tell me soon.

"I went home and looked in my kitchen, like Moonblood said, and there wasn't a damn thing there that isn't always there. But then I went to bed and I had this weird dream, about hanging up my clothes on a hook. Then when I got up, there it was—the hook, bigger than life, right in my kitchen, exactly like Moonblood said."

"What hook?"

"The one where I keep my extra keys—to the house, I mean. But there might—just very, very possibly might—have been a car key, too. The hook's behind the door, which I never close, so I didn't even notice they weren't there; I guess Pigball forgot to return them."

Her normally charming habit of forgetting names was

170

now up there—for irritation value—with guys who call you "doll." "May I ask which Pigball?"

"My friend Roxanne, who cat-sits when I go away for the weekend, or on vacation or something. I've known her forever—well, since high school, actually; she's from my hometown. We don't have much in common, but we've always kept in touch. Anyway, she's a free-lance something—editor, I think, and she does this kind of stuff for a few extra bucks. It's been nearly a year since I've been anywhere at all—but for all I know she's had the keys a lot longer; I never think about whether she does or doesn't have them because she's a good friend and I trust her—and I always know I'll be calling her again for the same job."

"Have you talked to her?"

"Her phone's disconnected." Seeing my fallen face, she said, "But not to worry. I have her mom's number in Virginia. I was just about to call when you came in."

"I've got to ask you something; I just have to. How could you forget your extra set of keys?"

She looked hurt. "Well first of all, in my mind they weren't missing. I just never thought—because they're always there, where they're supposed to be." She touched her long nose. "And second, they're house keys. I seem to have this dim, dim recollection of once putting a car key on the ring, so I'd have a complete set. But I don't know if I did it or just thought about it once or twice."

Kruzick, who'd been lurking in the doorway, trotted out his best Eddie Haskell voice: "May I make a suggestion? How about calling Roxanne's mother?"

"Roger," Chris said, and for obvious reasons the word made me laugh.

She dialed. "Mrs. Niekirk? Chris Nicholson. Oh, gosh, it has, hasn't it?"

Been a long time, I filled in, and hoped the pleasantries weren't going to go on at the normal Southern length.

Finally, she said, "I was wondering—I think Roxanne's moved and for some reason I don't have her phone number. Do you think—oh, she's there? Well, yes by all means." Pause. "Roxanne Niekirk, whatever do you think you're doing, leavin' town without tellin' me?" Her accent had kicked back to life. "Oh, hey. Darlin, what'd I say? Listen, I'm really, really sorry."

I gathered that Roxanne's reasons for leaving town weren't the happiest. But neither Kruzick, who by now had come in and sat down, nor I, were delicate enough to leave. We listened as Chris soothed her friend and then worked up to asking about the keys. Which apparently provoked a whole new flood of tears. Chris soothed a little bit more and then her end of the conversation began to tend more toward the occasional "uh-huh" or "yes", accompanied by alert nods and vigorous finger drumming; even note taking now and then.

After a time, she said, "I think I might have some bad news for you. Jason McKendrick died about a week ago."

Judging from what followed, Roxanne hadn't heard yet. But from Chris's sudden alertness, I knew we'd hit pay dirt. Yet when she finally hung up she hollered a loud and heartfelt, "Shit!"

"What is it?"

"You're not going to believe this. It's way too labyrinthine. You're just not gonna believe it." Long pause. "I don't know where to start."

Kruzick said, "The bottom line, as you Yanks so crudely put it, would be ever so appropriate, Mum."

"She left the keys in McKendrick's car."

"Shit!" Kruzick and I spoke together and then fell silent, staring into space.

Finally, I said, "I think the shock's worn off. You can hit us with the rest of it."

She drummed her desk again, something I'd never see her do before—an ugly habit, usually, but on Chris it looked good. She'd painted her nails a fetching Chinese red, and she was wearing a long-sleeved cream silk blouse. The long, long fingers, backed by silk-swathed wrists, tipped with red, were as elegant, even in her impatience, as a musical instrument.

"Roxanne's . . . how to say this . . . well, she's probably carrying about fifty more pounds than she'd like to be. She wears glasses; she's short; and she's shy. Now does she sound like a Jason McKendrick woman or what?"

"One kind, anyway."

"What a weird dude. I'm not kidding, it's a crime what he did to that girl. She wasn't making it as a free-lance editor, so about three months ago she went down to the *Chronicle* and applied for a job."

"Don't tell me." Kruzick was rolling his eyes. "She met him in the elevator."

"How'd you know that?"

"All the best lives are ruined that way. It's something about the motion." He wrinkled his nose. "And the slipping standards, of course. One day the Orient Express, the next elevators."

"Anyway, she was bowled over, she couldn't believe the likes of *him* could possibly be interested in *her*, and one day they left her house for a drink—at her insistence, after she'd been screwing him for about a month—and then she didn't hear from him for about a week and a half. Finally, he called and asked her if she'd dropped any keys in his car. Well, she didn't realize she had mine, so she said no, but she'd missed him and could they get together soon. So he dropped the news that he thought the relationship 'wasn't really going anywhere. . . .' "

"Men are swine," sniffed Kruzick.

"Anyway, she fell into a decline, and things began to get more and more desperate with her work situation. Meanwhile she actually got the *Chronicle* job she'd applied for, but she couldn't face McKendrick every day. Can you imagine? That poor girl.

"So finally she decided there wasn't anything left to do but go home to Virginia for a while and maybe try to find a job in Richmond or someplace like that. Anyhow, on just about the last day, she'd decided to treat herself to a movie all by herself, but the theater was in a neighborhood she wasn't crazy about, so she was putting money and things in a bellypack when this little heart fell out of her purse—a piece of the key ring I kept my extra keys on, and she realized she must have had my keys somewhere in her purse. When she couldn't find them, she knew she must have dropped them in McKendrick's car. So she decided to call him to tell him he had to send them to me and also give him a piece of her mind, kind of let him know what he put her through."

"What did he say?"

"Well, he was very cold and said he could certainly understand her position, or, as she put it, 'my fucking position,' and he was sorry things had worked out that way. And he took down my name and address."

"Eureka!" I shouted.

Kruzick said, "So how was the movie?"

We looked at him blankly.

"I mean, was she late because of the phone call, or did she bag it, or what?"

We ignored him.

I said, "It's over, do you realize that? Now we know why he had your name and address, and we know who had access to your car key."

"Yeah. The victim."

"How long was it between the time Roxanne said they weren't hers and the time she gave him your name?"

"I don't know. I had the impression it was a week, at least. Roxanne had to pack up to move, after all."

"Well, he could have done anything with them in the meantime. My guess is he did one of two things. Maybe he took them over to some woman's house—or even some other friend's house—thinking that person was the one who left them in his car. Then he later phoned to say they belonged to you and gave that person— henceforth known as the murderer—your name and address to mail them back. If she happened to be a woman scorned—especially recently scorned—she might have hatched a plan then and there. All she had to do was watch you and steal your car. Maybe she didn't mean to implicate you at all. Maybe she meant to sit in front of McKendrick's house until he came home, cream him, and then abandon the car wherever—no! She always meant to take it back to where you'd left it, because she had to park her own car there to save the space. So she must have known he'd be coming home when he was— but that would be easy enough. He was pals with most of his old girlfriends. She could just have asked him."

"What's the other thing he might have done?"

"Well, he might have left the keys in his glove box, and somebody who rode in his car picked them up for some reason—maybe just playing around—'Hey, Jase, can I have the key to your heart?'—who knows? And then later he phoned to say they were Chris's."

"Awfully damn responsible of him."

"Well, he was a complicated man."

"Right," said Kruzick. "He breaks a woman's heart and then to compensate, he has to take care of the little things like this, even gets obsessive about it. Maybe a little crazy."

I confess I turned and stared, openmouthed, never having imagined him capable of such insight.

"What?" He shrugged. "It's what I'd do."

Chris ignored us both, her mind on something else. "She said he had a brother."

"Who?"

"Jason. Did you know that?"

"Only the sister came to the wake."

"I know, that's why it's odd. She said, 'I wish he was gay like his brother.' That was before I told her he was dead. Apparently, she thought he was a menace. But then she was desperately in love again once she found out he was permanently unavailable."

"Ah, the human condition—don't you love it?" Kruzick got up to answer a ringing phone. "Rebecca, it's a Dr. Suzawa."

The surgeon, which meant bad news. The pathologist had called to tell him the worst. I knew this because he'd said I was to call to get the results. There was only one reason he'd call me.

"Hi there, how're you doing?"

"Fine, thanks." My throat was closing, but I got the words out. How could a man on such a mission ask a question like that? Surely Miss Manners would throw up her hands in horror.

"Well, I just thought you'd want to know. The biopsy was negative."

"But . . . you told me to call you."

"I always like to deliver good news."

A saint. A saint and an MD—not a natural combination.

"Wheeeeee! Drinks on the house!" I raced through the office like a madwoman. "In fact, let's all go out to dinner tonight. My treat. No, forget that—we can talk about the case and charge it to the office. Alan, get Mickey. And I'll ask Rob too. Yes, by all means."

Chris said, "Rebecca, you're babbling."

And Kruzick said, one hand on the phone, "What shall I tell Madame is the great occasion?"

"My biopsy was negative!"

His brow wrinkled. "What biopsy?"

But Chris came out to the reception area, shouting, "Hot damn!" and began to polka me around the office. And for three days after that Kruzick was on his best behavior, having gotten a taste of what it's like to share an office with lunatics.

Having hardly worked in a week, I figured now wasn't the time to start. I took the rest of the day off, dropping first by the Hall of Justice to give Martinez and Curry the glad tidings.

That is, I intended to take the rest of the day off. They kept me there, going over and over the story, calling Chris in, calling Roxanne in Virginia, carrying on as if we had nothing better to do than help them beat a dead horse.

That night at dinner Rob didn't seem half as thrilled about our hot new evidence as we were. There's not a doubt in my mind he wanted Chris cleared, but it didn't do much for his story.

But I was happy and Chris was happy—we both had plenty to celebrate; Mickey and Alan were ecstatic—they were getting a free meal at the Bravo Caffe; we all wanted Rob to be happy. So I made sure his wineglass was always full, and I gave him lots of attention and smiles. To be perfectly honest, I flirted with him, a somewhat dishonest proposition under the circumstances. If I hadn't had a glass or two myself I might have felt guiltier; as it was, I merely noticed it worked. He got into the spirit, and the five of us celebrated like guests at a Mafia wedding. Nothing was too trivial to laugh at; nothing too expensive to order.

I remembered a million other evenings like this—with Rob and me and Chris, sometimes with one of her boyfriends, or Mickey and Rob and me, with or without Kruzick—or the five of us together.

I remembered what I liked about Rob—his social ease, his cleverness, the way he could be so much fun when he hadn't disappeared for days on some story he'd forgotten to mention. I was starting to think that maybe, after all, Julio had reason to be jealous. I was so overcome with nostalgia and good feeling that I invited them all to my place for coffee.

We were laughing and probably talking way too loud—paying no attention to anything except our own good mood—and we had just begun the ascent to my apartment, up Green Street, when we heard the first shot. Almost as quickly, there was another. We could have jumped into a doorway if there'd been one, but there was nothing, no cover at all, in this section of the block, and now we heard clatter, footsteps behind us.

Like a herd of cattle, we began to stampede—all five at once, as if at a silent signal, simply took off hell-bent for leather.

"Shit!" Rob yelled behind me, and I looked back, saw him grasp his arm, and knew he was hit. Another second later we were all cowering in the overhang of my front door. There was no one behind us, and there were no more shots, though people were poking heads out of windows, even stepping outdoors, gathering to see what had happened. Not wanting to talk, I fumbled for my key and let us in.

"Rob, let's see."

"Winged my wing." He held up his right arm, showing a bullet hole in his jacket sleeve.

"Does it hurt?"

"Not yet. I must be in shock."

Quickly, before the pain started, he wrestled the jacket off, revealing one pristine arm, not so much as a wrist hair disturbed.

"Holy shit," said Mickey, and Rob, speechless for once, started to laugh. The rest of us caught it, and it was five minutes before we could climb the stairs to my apartment.

The shots meant another bout with Curry and Martinez, but there was no help for it. Instead of coffee, we had cognac, knowing the cops wouldn't be thrilled about it, but feeling an unaccustomed, un-nineties need for a stiff belt.

And as soon as Rob had fortified himself, he phoned in a little story, prompting Mickey to call our parents, knowing they'd get overexcited if they read it in the paper.

It was late before the dread detective duo had raked us over the coals and left. Mickey, Alan, and Chris left in a cluster, but Rob couldn't seem to make up his mind to go.

When I hinted, he said, "Rebecca. Someone tried to kill me." His voice was full of wonder.

We didn't know that, really—they could have been trying for any of us—but there was no denying he was the one they'd nearly gotten. I opened my arms to him, and we hugged for a long time. We kissed a little as well, but after a moment I resisted, and in time, he left, though I offered him the couch.

I thought, as I watched him go, that I'd never seen him look so sad. But his life was the one he had chosen, a life alone, a life of adventure yet no real closeness, and I couldn't change that.

When I was in bed, tears, seemingly from nowhere, trailed down my cheeks. I wanted to call Julio, but it was too late, and anyway, what would I say? "My biopsy's negative, but I got shot at"? It might not be the easiest thing to relate to, since I'd never gotten up the nerve to mention The Thing.

Even in my tears, I could have kicked myself. How could a person who couldn't tell her own boyfriend about a breast lump judge someone else's choice for aloneness?

CHAPTER 17

It's funny how a few hours' sleep can turn a grim world downright hospitable. That and the sun, I suppose. And maybe cheerful genes. I woke eager to get back to my regular schedule, more or less convinced we'd been set upon by a random lunatic, which I suppose made me a candidate for one myself.

I breezed into the office and buried myself under a pile of paper, hardly wincing when I heard my mother's voice on the phone. Of course I had to know she'd call—no serious mom lets it go by when both her daughters get shot at. But she didn't mention the usual stuff—why didn't I be more careful, maybe move back to Marin, that sort of thing. She galloped right into strange and uncharted territory, sort of the badlands of the morning coffee break.

"Rebecca, I have a message for you. I called, like I do every third Thursday, for my Tarot reading and—"

"Mom? Is this Sondra Schwartz? Excuse me, is this the mother of Rebecca Schwartz?"

"Could I ask what's going on, please?"

"*Tarot?* You? My mother?" I was sputtering, but I guess that was part of the message.

"I never mentioned it to you?"

"I really think I'd remember."

"Well, it's no big deal, I just get a Tarot reading once a month."

My world was fast falling apart. "Hold it, could we back up a little? How long has this been going on? And what's this about calling for a reading? You did say that, didn't you? How on earth can you get a Tarot reading on the phone?"

"Well . . ." She paused, incredulity in her voice. What could she say to a Venusian? "On the psychic line."

How else? her voice implied, but I was pretty sure I must have just entered the Twilight Zone. "*The psychic line?* That thing on television? But it's so . . . but, Mom, it's so . . ."

"Dumb?"

That wasn't the half of it. Its commercials were apparently geared to ladies with big hair and permanent seats on bar stools in country-western bars, ladies who pined for love first and money second. Mom had enough of both, I would have thought, plus a keen enough interest in the present to let the future alone.

"Well, I know it doesn't seem like a Marin kind of thing, but my friend Suzanne, who's got insomnia and stays up watching late-night TV, just couldn't resist one night. She says it does weird things to you, spending eight hours a day with a television set. So she called the psychic line and that's how we discovered Maurizio. He reads the Tarot—have you ever seen a Tarot deck?"

"Mom, I went to school in Berkeley. Who on Earth is Maurizio?"

"He's a brilliant psychic. Really sort of a genius."

I should get him and Chris together. I blurted, "What kinds of questions do you ask?"

"Thereby hangs a tale. Sometimes I ask about you and Mickey and Daddy. So he knows all your names and everything—quite a bit about you, to tell you the truth.

"Well, today I called and asked about you, you know, what happened last night; and I thought he sounded different from usual. He gave me a pretty humdrum reading, I thought, but he sounded excited. Does that make any sense?"

"I guess so." Though of course it didn't.

"Well, he asked for my phone number, which he's never done before. I mean, I have to call him. Anyway, he called back in about half an hour, and he said, 'Have your daughter call me.' "

"Oh, Mom, you've got to be kidding."

"No, really, that's what he said."

"For a *reading*? The guy wants me to call him for a Tarot reading?" The whole world had gone nuts.

"Well, I'm not sure, but I think you should call him. You see, naturally I thought this thing with Chris and Jason McKendrick had something to do with your getting shot at."

"Maybe so."

"Well, Maurizio and I got to chatting, and it turns out he knows Jason McKendrick's brother."

I'd been leaning back in my chair, front feet off the ground. I came back down to Earth with a thump. "He does? What's his number?"

She reeled off one with a 404 area code.

"Where's that?"

"Atlanta."

So I called him. If the beyond had sent me a message, who was I not to sign up for it?

"Maurizio La Fabio? Rebecca Schwartz."

"Ah, Rebecca. You have the most delightful mother." Already he knew something I didn't.

"'She said I should phone you."

"Oh, yes. I read your cards. Very interesting. Very, very interesting, if I do say so."

I wondered if I should offer to cross his palm with silver.

"But, in the long run, not half as interesting as Michael." He sighed. "I used to go out with him."

"I'm—ah—losing the thread."

"Oh, sorry. I was just taking one of those unexpected little strolls down memory lane. Does that ever happen to you?"

"I guess it happens to everybody." Exactly what, I didn't know, but bonding was the thing here. Maurizio and I should be pals, I thought, or he'd never reveal the secrets of the psychic line.

"Michael is Jason's brother. Michael Mckendrick."

"Oh, yes. Mom said you knew him. Was he here when Jason died? I don't remember meeting him."

"No, and he was horribly broken up about it. You see, Michael's a hugely talented but wildly unlucky musician—well, actually I've done his chart (I'm an astrologer too), and there's nothing surprising about it. And anyway he's barely passed his Saturn return yet. Things should improve for him soon. Anyway, for once Michael had a gig. I mean a whole week of pretty good gigs—a little tour arranged six months before—and if things had been going better, I know he'd have been the first one there." He sighed again. "Poor, poor baby. He just didn't think he could do it. And he's *destroyed*. He's been absolutely wrecked ever since."

"He and Jason were close?"

"I wouldn't put it that way, exactly. You have to let Michael tell you. He needs this. I'm telling you; he needs it desperately."

"He needs what?"

"To talk to you. To clear this thing up."

"Hold it. You're saying Michael knows who killed Jason?"

"Of course not. He'd have gone to the police if he did. Common sense would tell you that. Look. Here's the thing. You need to see him. It's in the cards."

"I thought you said Michael needed this. Who needs whom here?"

"You need each other. It's a match made in heaven, Sunshine. Can you get a plane out today?"

"I'm a little overwhelmed, to tell you the truth. Could you tell me exactly what the cards said?"

"They said Michael was going to be very important in your life."

Oh, no. Shades of the Cosmic Blind Date.

"But only briefly. You only have one thing to do together, as far as I can tell."

"Did you say you used to go out with Michael?"

"Yes. Why?"

"He's gay then?"

"Completely."

"Not bisexual?"

"He doesn't even talk to his own sister."

Who would if they could avoid it? But I said, "That sounds safe enough."

Maurizio burst out laughing. "Believe me, it wasn't *that* kind of reading. Michael would rather die."

"Well, look, have you talked to Michael at all? Will he see me?"

"Michael's out of town right now, but of course he'll see you. You don't think he'd let you come all this way for nothing, do you?"

Sure I did. It was the most harebrained scheme I ever heard in my life. "Well, look, Maurizio, I'll think about it."

"Talk to your partner about it."

But that would have to wait. As I hung up, it was not my partner who came barreling through the door, but Rob, closely followed by Kruzick, who was rubbing his hands and hunched over. "Oh, Missie Rebecca, I try to stop Impetuous One. I tell him like always the Queen is in meeting, and he chops off three of humble servant's fingers." I didn't have the least idea who he was supposed to be.

Rob said, "Adrienne's missing," and plopped into my client's chair. Kruzick withdrew cackling, as pleased with himself as if we'd given him five curtain calls.

"What do you mean missing? I thought she was still in a coma."

"I guess she woke up yesterday afternoon—that's what they're saying at the hospital, but for all I know this is a story they made up on the spur of the moment. They moved her out of intensive care, her dad went to see her, and she was gone."

"Checked out?"

"Uh-uh. Like I said—disappeared."

"Were her clothes missing?"

"Oh, yes. It looked a lot like she got out under her own steam."

"I wouldn't think she'd have a lot after a few days in a coma."

"You wouldn't, would you? They did make the point that she ate heartily almost as soon as she woke up. I guess she was stoked, as the young people say."

"I think that means something else. She woke up yesterday afternoon?"

He nodded again.

"So when did she disappear?"

"That's the question, all right. Not at all long after. About three o'clock, they figure. She'd have had plenty of time to shoot us—and no way at all of knowing you and Chris were out of it. Of course, I still think the shooter was aiming at me. Most of the people we've seen never even asked who you are, and I'm the one writing the worrisome stories."

A thought occurred to me. "What about Chris? What if the person who framed her doesn't want to let her off the hook?"

His face sobered quickly. "Oh, shit."

I agreed with him.

"Look," he said, "I think I know who Adrienne's ex-boyfriend is—Danno, I mean."

"And you didn't tell me before?"

He turned slightly red. "Well, it was kind of like Chris and the key—I just didn't put it together. There was this copyboy named Daniel—you know how people like that can kind of be invisible? It shouldn't be, but it is, especially if there's an age gap. You kind of only see people your own age. I don't know how long he was there, but he's been gone awhile—at least three or four months. Today I heard a couple of copyboys talking while I was getting coffee, and they kept saying, 'Danno.' Danno goes to a lot of South of Market clubs and reports on them, apparently. So it was something on the order of, 'Danno says the Skullcap is only good on Fridays, but Eraserhead's rockin' every night.' Not exactly riveting for your over-thirty stay-at-home, and I hadn't had my coffee yet. But even in my unswift state, after the third or fourth 'Danno,' a bell started ringing somewhere off in the distance. Anyhow, I made inquiries. His name is Daniel Piperis, and yes, he and Adrienne used to be an item. He now works as a bike messenger, and every day at lunchtime goes to hang out with the other messengers at the corner of Market and Sutter, by the Sharper Image."

I looked at my watch: eleven-forty. "Meet you there in fifteen minutes."

"If you get there first, he'll be the one with the dreads."

"Piperis is black?"

"Piperis is pretending."

The bike messengers in San Francisco are an institution we all hope the fax machine won't destroy. They're known for their daredevil ways, utter disregard for convention, and flair for fashion statements. When I got there, I saw Rob watching from across the street. There was only one guy with dreads, and he wore two pairs of shorts, one on top of the other, each in a different plaid, topped with a short-sleeved shirt in yet a third. I was willing to bet when he wasn't on a bike, you could find him on a skateboard.

"The chap in the McKendrick tartan?" I said.

"Tasteless. Unworthy of you. Let's go get him." He hollered, "Yo, Danno," something I'd never have done, considering the kid might have something big to hide. But he didn't take off, instead waited politely.

"The great Rob Burns," he said. "Don't tell me, it's a nationwide talent hunt for the next Herb Caen."

"We're looking for Adrienne Dunson."

He did what was very nearly a classic double take. "Adrienne. I haven't seen her in months. Adrienne! What was I thinking of? I wasn't—it was all her idea." Most of this speech was delivered more or less staring off into space. He came back into focus. "Sorry. I talk to myself. It's one of the things she didn't like about me."

"Well, there's some bad news and some good news. I might as well say it fast. The good news is that she's up and around. The bad news is she took sleeping pills a few days ago. She was in a coma for a while. And then she disappeared from the hospital. You didn't know any of this?''

"God, no.'' He certainly looked stunned, whether he was or not. "No. I didn't know any of it. Did she say why?''

"She's gone missing, Danno. We thought she might have gone to stay with you.''

He looked sheepish. "She left messages. I guess I just kind of ignored them.''

"I take it you parted acrimoniously.''

"I don't know what the deal is with Adrienne. She grew up in a family where one kid was desperately, desperately ill. I'm not sure what was wrong with him, but something; the whole family revolved around the kid's illness. Adrienne would say things like, 'We weren't in denial or anything; it was just a part of life.' Like every family lived with that. Like nobody ever told her how awful it was; especially the way no one paid any attention to her. I mean, I guess that's what happened; I don't know.'' He got the spacey look again, and then his eyes came in for a landing. "The upshot is, that's the coldest bitch I ever met in my life. The day I let her stay with me I'd have to be the one in a coma.''

"Wow. Strong stuff.''

"It was like she'd think of ways to get me pissed off. To make an enemy out of me, really. And she couldn't have been more amazed when I told her to leave. She said, 'But we're such a great fit. We like all the same bands and movies and everything.' Like she never noticed a damn thing was wrong.'' He spread his hands. "I guess she was friends with McKendrick; I don't know. Maybe he was just nice to her for old times' sake.''

"Wait a minute. Are you saying they were an item before she came to the *Chronicle*?"

"Oh, God no. I mean, I guess not, I never even thought about it. He was pushing forty, I guess—" He stopped, mused, and shook his head. "Uh-uh. No way. But their families had been friends for centuries or something."

This was more interesting still.

"They, you know, grew up together, sort of. Or I guess they would have if he hadn't been a whole generation older."

I'd like to think it was that conversation that most influenced my decision to fly to Atlanta. As Rob said when we had left Danno, he made Adrienne sound like a classic psychopath—definitely not someone you wanted gunning for you. Maybe, I thought, I could uncover the hidden motive, the ancient reason she'd finally had enough and run Jason down, and Martinez and Curry would pull out all the stops. I already had a theory to fit the keys—one so natural and obvious, it had to be right. Adrienne was after all Jason's assistant—he'd probably given her Chris's keys and asked her to return them. Adrienne had copied down her address—maybe he'd even read it off to her, on the telephone, perhaps—and he'd absentmindedly returned his own scrap to his pocket.

I did what Maurizio said, talked to my partner about going to Atlanta. She responded by closing her eyes and checking it out.

And so I cling to Danno; otherwise I'd be a person who had once more agreed—even after two dates with a flying saucer enthusiast—to meet someone because a gang of roving psychics thought it was a fine idea.

CHAPTER 18

It was good for me to go to Atlanta. I hadn't been before, and I found it humbling. There is just the tiniest tendency on the part of someone from San Francisco to imagine that she is sophisticated, cosmopolitan, a woman of the world, and that a person from Atlanta may be just a trifle less worldly wise. Five minutes in the Atlanta airport should dispel such fantasies.

In case there is anyone who hasn't yet been—which I doubt, as I was told by the natives I was the last—you have to take a train to get from one concourse to another and said train, like those en route to the Interplanetary Council, travels at the speed of thought. Already it's like science fiction, and you might just lean back to take it all in. Whereupon the train will scold you in a robot voice: "You are being delayed because someone has interfered with the doors closing. As soon as the doors close, we will depart." I hear there's an airport in Sarasota that's similar; maybe there are more. I'm sure Roger DeCampo wouldn't be half so strange if computers didn't run trains.

I couldn't figure out exactly how the thing is built, but what I think is that most of the airport is underground, and so you get that odd molelike feeling you get in a casino, with no windows, only artificial light, and a general sense, in my case at least, of claustrophobia and depression; even, sometimes, a bit of desperation, the sort of thing spelunkers report when their candles go out.

Somewhere, somehow, after a ten- or twenty-mile journey from the gate, with robots yelling at me and my eyes trying to adjust to the dimness, I spotted a familiar sight—my own name hand-lettered on a piece of cardboard.

The person holding it can only be described as a hunk—about six-feet-two, shoulders like Atlas, and a face that reminded me a little of Richard Gere. He wore shorts and an open-necked polo shirt. A lightning bolt on a chain nestled into thick, lovely chest hair.

"Maurizio?" I hadn't expected a Tarot reader to be so physical.

"Rebecca. I'd know you anywhere."

"You'd know me? How could you know me? Surely you aren't that psychic."

"Oh, but I am. I closed my eyes, and I pictured you exactly. Only I thought you'd have red hair."

My hair is dark, my eyes brown, my skin close to olive; surely if I had red hair I'd have green or blue eyes and pink or gold skin—in other words, I could hardly look more different. I said, "Two eyes, two arms, that sort of thing."

"No, really, I got your height and build exactly. And the hairstyle."

"No fair on the hairstyle—everyone wears their hair like this nowadays." Side-parted, shoulder-length—my hairdresser calls it the "triangle."

"Not your sister. She still has long, thick, seventies hair; cascades of non-nineties curls."

"Mom told you that."

"Nope. She sent me a picture. She thought I could focus better that way."

Who the hell was my mom, anyway? This was almost as confusing as Chris's confession.

We had arrived by now at Maurizio's car, and he announced that he was taking me to my hotel, where I would be left alone until dinnertime, when Michael McKendrick would arrive to take me to dinner—at Maurizio's.

"You're kidding," I said. "All this and you're cooking, too?

He shrugged. "Just some chicken and a few amusing little Cuban dishes. Most of it I made for my last dinner party and froze the leftovers."

"Come on. You're going to a lot of trouble."

"I like Michael even if he did dump me. And anyway, it's part of the job."

I stared out the window and thought you'd never guess from the cool coccoon of the car that it was a blast furnace out there. They called freeways expressways here. Did I feel free to express my doubts?

Finally, I said, "You mean psychics have to take care of perfect strangers from three thousand miles away?"

"I like to help people. This job has been good to me." There was infinite dignity in the way he said the simple words, not a wasted one in the bunch. He didn't look at me, kept his eyes on the road, just spoke as if stating he enjoyed eggs for breakfast.

"Do you make a living at it?"

"Reading the cards?"

He shrugged. "I'm a gardener, too—or I was. Right now I'm mostly a caregiver—a sort of nurse—for someone who's very ill. I take my psychic line calls at his house. You see, I can do both jobs at once, and it almost adds up to one good job. And I do the nursing for love; it's an old friend who's dying. I'm all he has left now, and he can pay me something, but not much. With the psychic line I can do it.''

''That's how the job has been good to you?'' Maybe he was a saint, but then again maybe he was just a little too good to be true.

''Oh, no, it got me out of Miami. You know how ugly that town is right now? Anyway, I wanted to come here because my parents moved here a few years ago—couldn't take it down there anymore. But I had a good business—a gardening business with five employees and three trucks. I was afraid to move. But the psychic line gave me something to tide me over, just enough, till I could get going here. And I did some good readings for myself. I knew I had to come here.''

For the first time, he looked at me. ''I forgot something, I realized. I didn't read the cards until I got the job.''

''What, you're an amateur?''

''Hey, you have it or you don't.''

''But what happened? Why did you apply for a job you didn't know how to do?''

''I didn't. I got into it the same way you got to me—through my mother. I guess I should really start at the beginning. My mother read cards when I was a kid. This isn't Cuban, you know, but she learned it—it went with the other stuff she did. Santeria, you know what that is?''

''I don't think so.''

''A kind of magic. A funny religion that came to Cuba from Africa. Or, that is, it wasn't Santeria then, but it got all mixed up with Christianity. Like voodoo—you know voodoo?''

''Not intimately.''

''But you know what it is?''

"Haitian magic, I guess. I don't know much about it."

"And you probably don't want to, right? It gives you the creeps. How would you like it if your mother had a secret altar in a closet and you were always finding eggs sunk in weird liquids and stuff like that? Believe me, we kids were grossed out. And embarrassed. How unassimilated can you get, huh?

"But all Cubans do it, I'm convinced of it: at least all the women. They go to church on Sunday, and then they go home and make an offering to their saint."

"Saint? That isn't Christian?"

"See, Santeria and Christianity are mixed up, like I said. The santeros call them saints, but really, they're Yoruba deities. See this?" He dangled the lightning bolt around his neck. "My mom gave it to me. It means I'm a child of Chango, a black, male deity. But if you opened my mother's secret closet, you'd find a statue of Santa Barbara there. That's Chango also—the early practitioners had to disguise what they were doing."

I could imagine.

"Well, anyway, I'm off the subject. I just meant to say I grew up a little weird—at least compared to the other kids. We always had magic around the house, and so when my mother learned the Tarot it was just another thing. By the way, the Santeros have all kinds of divination, but you have to go to a professional and pay money. I guess Mom got tired of it. Anyway, the cards weren't even half as weird as most of the stuff she did. I was just a little kid and wanted to see what Mom did, so she taught me. And I was damned good, too—right away I was good. In fact, I was a lot better than she was. Like I said, you have it or you don't. But of course a boy couldn't do stuff like that. The other kids might find out. So I quit and forgot all about it. You're not going to believe what happened next.''

"Your mother called the psychic line and the psychic said have your son call me.''

He turned around and stared so long I feared for our safety. "How'd you know that? I never told your mother.''

I shrugged. "Lucky guess.'' Then I got pleased with myself. "Is that it? Really?''

"Oh, well, I guess it was easy. Anyway, I started reading, and I got popular, so they gave me a raise and pretty soon I got out of Miami. So I guess the moral is listen to your mama.''

"That's what I'm doing here. Listen, what makes one Tarot reader better than another?''

He looked uncomfortable. "I wish I knew. I just get the right cards, that's all. But also I know things. I don't know how I do, but I do. See, that's the spooky part. I don't know if the cards cue what I know or if I magically turn up the right cards. Maybe it's something in the fingertips—energy, I mean. Something.''

"You never had any formal training?''

"Just from my mom.'' He looked surprised. "You mean there's schools you can go to or something?''

"I don't know.'' No sense mentioning Rosalie.

He dropped me, and I read a murder mystery while I waited for dinner—I was way too keyed up to sleep, but grateful for the psychic respite, you should excuse the expression.

I'd been told dinner would be casual, so I pulled out a pair of flowered shorts and a T-shirt. I wished for some sandals but had to make do with Nikes. At seven I was ready, and at seven Michael arrived. If Maurizio had surprised me with his glamour, Michael shocked me with his ordinariness. I had never seen Jason, but I had seen their sister, and I was prepared, I guess, for something along the lines of a dragon rampant—not an unfriendly one, just a creature you'd notice.

Michael had all too obviously taken to heart the warnings about using sunscreen. Or perhaps, owing to being a musician, he didn't get out much before sunset. He had longish brownish thinning hair, which he wore in a ponytail, and he was average height, but a little chubs. His face was apple-round, his features heavy—more or less nondescript—and pale as a petal. I wondered why the magnificent Maurizio carried a torch for him. He wore cut-off khakis and a vintage shirt, something from the fifties, I thought, quietly chic in an Atlanta that probably wouldn't notice, if other clothes I saw were any indication.

He shook my hand vigorously, pumped it good, but didn't really say much other than "Hi."

He helped me into a brown Blazer and got back on the ubiquitous expressway. "Maurizio's condo's near Sandy Springs. Hardly anyone lives in town, you know."

"This place is a little like L.A., isn't it?"

"Not really," he said, but didn't elaborate.

"I meant, you know, all freeways and malls."

He nodded. "Mmm."

It was going to be a long ride. I decided to get through it by looking out the window. Which afforded lots of great views of cars.

Finally I got up the nerve to say, "I didn't know your brother, but he was a terrific writer. Everyone thought so."

He said, "Thank you. We aren't a close family."

I went back to the cars.

Maurizio lived in quite a snazzy condo, which, he explained, was possible because he had a roommate (tactfully out for the evening). The feature I liked best was a perfect little backyard, where Maurizio was barbecuing chicken.

Michael headed straight for the refrigerator, silently removed two beers, and handed one to me. Though I'm not much of a beer drinker, I certainly wasn't going to argue. I popped my top and swigged.

But Maurizio was scandalized, "Don't drink those filthy things. Let's have fuzzy navels."

I don't know if this is a nationally known drink, but I later questioned a number of San Franciscans who'd never heard of it. It's a drink ideally suited to Georgia, thoroughly refreshing in the heat; kind of a screwdriver with a Southern accent. I've never been quite sure, but I think the ingredients are vodka, orange juice (the navel part), and peach schnappes (the fuzz). The result is peachy keen.

As we sipped, the guys talked sports for a while and exchanged tidbits about mutual friends. Michael polished off his fuzzy navel and helped himself to another. His color changed as he drank, grew pinker and friendlier, along with his demeanor. He was shy, perhaps, and drank consciously to loosen up. More likely, I think, he was hostile to me, to the idea of talking about his brother; he'd been roped into the evening, and was oiling up for the ordeal. Maurizio was quite the operator, I thought, remembering I'd flown three thousand miles myself. I still didn't see what he saw in Michael, but I was getting an idea why Michael would dump him—the man was dangerous.

But heck. He barbecued a mean chicken, which he served with salad—a green one with lots of avocado—black beans and rice, and fried plantains. For dessert he'd made key lime pie. Throughout dinner he kept up a three-way conversation, no small feat considering Michael's wariness.

By the time we'd made a good-sized dent in the pie, Michael knew pretty much about my family—my mom, who gets her Tarot read, my sister Mickey, who's sweet as a sundae and works for Planned Parenthood, my dad the famous defense lawyer, and my sister's boyfriend, the ne'er-do-well actor. It was Kruzick that won him over, I think—the fact that I had to put up with him in my office. Suddenly I had all his sympathy. Either that or the fuzzy navels had done their work. He was smiling at me now, even sometimes, in a fit of wild abandon, addressing the odd remark to me. Maurizio began to lead him skillfully to the matter at hand.

"Listen, Michael, you know what we talked about."

He sobered. "Yeah." And looked down at his plate.

"Let me get you another drink."

When he looked up, he had tears in his eyes. "I don't think I can tell the story without it."

When he had a new drink—this time a bourbon and water—and had drunk a few sips of it, he said, "This thing tore our family apart. It's like, really, really hard to talk about. I was fourteen when it happened, and I had this big brother that I more or less worshipped and then, like *boom*, the whole thing was shattered. Everything. Tressa was twelve. She, like, never even acknowledges the rest of us anymore. And our parents more or less disowned Jason. He was out on the streets, practically, right afterward. We tried to keep in touch, but, I don't know. . . ." He took a big swallow of the drink and put it down. "After that, nothing was normal. And it never will be again."

Maurizio said, "Okay, you were fourteen, Jason was eighteen, and Tressa was twelve. You were all together when it happened?"

"Well, it was summer, and Jason was about to leave for college. I think he thought he might miss us, or he'd never have let us go with him. See, he was the only one who could drive, and he said, come on, let's take Max for a walk above Inspiration Point. It was, like, a Saturday afternoon; maybe a Sunday. There were a whole lot of people out." He winced slightly and went quiet for a while. "Anyway, he'd never done anything like that before. Never! Tres and I thought we'd died and gone to heaven."

"Inspiration Point?" I asked. "You lived in the Bay Area?"

He nodded. "You know Inspiration Point? In Tilden?"

"I haven't been there in a long time."

"Well, there's this great paved path that goes up and down over hills and everything. It used to be a road to a missile site, and it's really wide—people can walk three or four abreast. Anyway, people walk their dogs up there and some people bicycle. That's what the problem was."

"I beg your pardon?"

"Well, to make a long story short, you're supposed to keep your dogs on their leashes, right? You know how that is?"

"Uh-huh."

"Well, Jason didn't. Max was this really hyper dog, and he said it was because Max never got to run and who cared anyway? So he let him off the leash and a rabbit or something hopped across the road, and Max just took off. We kept calling him, but he wouldn't come back, he was just way too excited—there were other dogs around and everything. Well, anyway, there was this man on a bicycle with a little infant seat on the back. You know those things? You've got to remember this was a long time ago—I don't even know if they made those little helmets then. But anyway this kid wasn't wearing one.

"I don't know. I just don't know how it could have happened. Max just wasn't paying attention, and he crashed into the bike. The father . . ."

His face turned into a tragedy mask as he remembered. "You should have seen the look of panic on that father's face. I thought he was going to turn himself inside out to keep the bike upright. But it went down, and I swear to God I'll never forget the noise it made as long as I live, when Sean hit the pavement. When his head hit."

"Sean was the baby?"

"Yeah. That was his name."

The horror of it flooded in on me. I imagined what it was like to be fourteen and see something like that and to know that your big brother was responsible—that *you* were—because there was no way at that age you could ever convince yourself it wasn't your fault. It was your brother, it was your dog; it must be your fault.

"He was killed?" I said, making it more a statement than a question.

"Oh, no. Oh God, if only he'd been killed. He was horribly brain-damaged and lived nearly eighteen years, more or less as a vegetable. But a walking vegetable—one who had seizures all the time. He could only say a few words, and couldn't take things in, couldn't learn, but he could walk, sort of. If you could call it that. He was all crippled and spastic. He had to wear diapers, which somebody had to change. And you just never knew when he was going to fall over with a seizure. Oh God, it was horrible." He tossed back the rest of his drink. I could understand the need to anesthetize himself; I was feeling pretty raw just hearing about it, not having to see it again in my mind's eye, to hear that awful noise.

He held up his empty glass, but Maurizio didn't offer another. "Sean Dunson died eight months ago at the age of eighteen—exactly the age Jason was when it happened. And that was horrible, too. I know every goddam detail. He had a little virus, and his temperature went way up, which caused a series—*series*, please—of uncontrolled seizures. Somehow in the midst of all that, he 'aspirated,' as the doctors say, and got pneumonia, which killed him. About eighteen years too late to save the Dunsons and the McKendricks."

He sat in bleakness, his head down, and his hands, wrapped around the glass, between his legs. "His parents seemed decent enough, I think. I don't really know, I was just a little kid. But I think they finally sued, and the suit didn't come to anything—our parents didn't really have any money; they gave them what they did have, which was Jason's college money. He went two years to a community college; that was all. The rest of us—Tres and I—didn't go at all, and everything was just . . . sad. After that. I don't remember ever being happy again, ever laughing in that house, ever even having a Christmas tree.

"Tressa started wearing all black as soon as she got to junior high, and Mom and Dad kind of . . ." He paused, trying, I thought, to figure out exactly what had happened to them. "They just gave up, I guess. Dad was an accountant but not a very successful one. Sometimes Mom would get a job in a bookstore. They'd worked really, really hard just to get through, and they never had extra money again. If they had money for Tres and me—for college—I guess they felt they had to give it to the Dunsons. I don't know for sure; I just know they were never the same again."

"And Jason?"

"I don't know. He never would say. He always seemed so upbeat, like he had everything under control, but I don't think he ever even began to get over it. For one thing, he got more distant, too—not like Tressa, who just checked out—but, I don't know, it was like none of us had much to say to each other after that. Like the shame of it was some big tent that collapsed on us and got us all tangled up, so we couldn't move anymore. Like if we looked at each other, we'd see Max crashing into that bike or something; we'd remember it. I think Jason gave the Dunsons money sometimes, but I'm not sure. We never talked about that." He looked away. "Do you know how much it costs to take care of somebody like that? It's a black hole that sucks your money into it."

The name Dunson was starting to ring a bell. I said, "Did you meet them? The Dunsons?"

"Oh God, yes. There were endless negotiations. And Mom was always trying to be nice—going to see Sean and everything. I went with her once or twice."

"Were there any other kids?"

"A little girl. I guess she was about five at the time."

"Adrienne? Was that her name?"

"How did you know about her?"

"She was Jason's assistant. You didn't know that?"

"How would I know that?" He sounded angry. "Maurizio, please?" He held up his glass again.

Maurizio took it, filled it, and looked at me apologetically. "I'll take you home," he said. "I don't think Michael better drive."

I said to Michael, "Was that the whole family? Just the parents and Adrienne?"

He nodded.

"Adrienne came with her dad to Jason's wake. I thought you'd like to know that."

"Tres and Jason went to Sean's funeral a few months ago. The Dunsons and the McKendricks. Just one big happy family." He drank, and then he said, "I wonder why Mrs. Dunson wasn't there."

"I guess I have more bad news for you. She committed suicide about six months ago. It must have been after Sean died."

His eyes seemed to sink deeper, so that he looked more miserable than ever. "Jason never told me. That was the way he was, he never talked about anything that worried him. But, man, he couldn't keep quiet about Sean's funeral. He was, like, *wrecked* by it. He said she was real thin—Mrs. Dunson. Real fragile-looking, shoulders shaking the whole time. He knew her before, knew what she looked like, I mean. He said it was like seeing a ghost."

CHAPTER 19

Back at the other end, Chris met me at the airport. I wasted no time: "I have news. Lots of it and all concerning Adrienne. Has she turned up yet?"

"Afraid not."

"She's scary as hell, Chris. The thing she had with McKendrick—you're not going to believe how sick it was. Sick and manipulative." I told her the story Michael had told.

"Adrienne had this incredible power over him," she said. "I guess he felt so guilty he'd do anything she wanted. 'Hire me.' 'Sure.' 'Let me move in.' 'No problem.' And who knows what else? Maybe he gave her money, too."

"Michael thinks he gave some to the Dunsons. It would certainly explain his vow of poverty."

"How about the vow of chastity?"

"There's a question, huh? I don't know if we'll ever get to the bottom of it, but one thing's obvious. This was a guy who was eaten up with guilt. That's what his whole life was about. Guilt. Being manipulated by Adrienne. Giving everything he made to the Dunsons. Not being able to get on with it. I think that whole A Team/B Team thing was about that. He wanted the A-Team women, but he didn't think he deserved them."

She gave me a weird look and started to focus.

"Chris, please don't close your eyes while you're driving."

"Oh, don't worry. It just sounded so right I was seeing if I could get a little open-eye hit."

"Did you?"

"Well, no. I'll try it later with my eyes closed. Anyway, it might have been more than that. Maybe he didn't consciously think he didn't deserve them. Maybe his body made certain decisions for him."

"Meaning he couldn't get it up."

"Meaning exactly that."

"But what he did with the B Team was pretty cruel."

"Well, maybe he didn't feel too good about it. He did have that episode with Tami the prostitute. Maybe he was trying to see if that would work."

"I guess it didn't, though."

"The women he did get involved with were broken wings, just like him. I don't know what a shrink would do with that."

"Well, I think I can almost get it," I said. "If he identified with them, then they were bound to keep getting hurt. Because that was his life."

She shrugged. "I don't know. But that couldn't-get-it-up business sure sounds likely. I mean—"

I laughed and finished for her, "Knowing men and all."

But the other part would remain forever as mysterious to us as it had probably been to Jason.

"What in the hell are we going to do about Adrienne?" she said.

"Well, I don't know that we have to do anything. The cops are probably looking for her already. If they aren't now, they will be after we tell them what Michael said."

"Actually, uh—could you indulge me?"

I was getting a sinking feeling. "Indulge you how?"

"I had the group read about it. I think we have to find her."

"Why?"

"I don't know why. They said it was the right action."

I didn't say anything, thinking it through.

"I'm involved in this thing, and I can't just drop out. She committed murder with my car, and she tried to frame me. I can't explain it exactly—it's not revenge or anything—I just need to bring the thing full circle."

Well, hell. I had crazy obsessions too—usually involving far more trivial matters than this one. "Far be it from me," I said, "to argue with the cosmos."

"Thanks." Her shoulders sagged, signaling how tense they'd been, how much she'd needed me to say yes.

"There's only one thing—we don't know where to look. Or did the Raiders tell you?"

"I wish."

"Well, let's go get some cappuccino and see if it jogs anything."

"You lawyers. Drugs, drugs, drugs." I didn't see her arguing, though.

The stuff didn't make us brilliant, but it did get us jump-started.

Assessing what we had to go on, there were only two possible leads—Adrienne's dad and Danno. Since her dad had reported her missing, it didn't seem likely he was hiding her. So Danno first, if we could find him. We called Rob for his address, but he wasn't home.

In that case, there was one thing to do—go back to Adrienne's apartment, the one she'd shared with Jason, and look for a Rolodex. Rob and I had broken in once before, and I had no doubt I could do it again.

Chris was appalled but invaluable at boosting me through the window, which, in the excitement, no one had thought to board up. She climbed in after me, and our noses told us immediately that this was an unlived-in place, a place starting to mildew and settle into its own bacterial, mossy smells. A quick check revealed we were right—if Adrienne had been back, there was no sign of it.

There was no Rolodex, though, either in the bedroom or the living room. Impatient, I went into the kitchen to call Rob again on the wall phone in there. A list of ten numbers programmed into the phone had been stuck neatly underneath a plastic envelope provided on the receiver. Number One was "Jason at work," Number Two was "Dad," and Number Three was "Danno."

"Eureka!" I shouted, but didn't yet press the button. This was delicate—required face-to-face contact—and I wasn't at all sure he'd simply invite us over.

"I've got it," said Chris, grabbing the receiver and pressing the button. "Hi," she said, "is this Daniel, uh . . . Piperis. Is the last name right? I couldn't quite read it. This is UPS, and we have a package for you, but it looks as if it got wet—the ink's so smeared we can't make out the address.

"Where's it from? Let me look again. New York, it looks like." Short pause. "Well, I can't read that either. Look, do you want the package or not? . . . Okay." She gestured for a pencil and took down an address. For a minute I thought she was going to have the chutz-pah to ask directions, but she hung up. "What a grouch. But no one can resist a mysterious package."

"Let's get out of here."

It would certainly have been no shock to me to learn that Danno lived in a loft South of Market, but in fact he inhabited a shabby building not far from Chinatown and cheek by jowl with the Tenderloin, a slightly un-savory area that drew people who were new in town, who hadn't much money or time to find a better place.

Sleepily, he said, "I'll be right down," and when he appeared he looked like someone who'd just gotten home from a rave and hadn't yet come down from it. He said, "Oh. I thought you were UPS."

"We're looking for Adrienne."

"I remember you. Look, I already told you—I don't know where she is."

"Danno, remember telling us about her brother? The one who was so ill?"

"Sure; Sean. Adrienne and I were together when he died. She was real, real upset about that."

"We think she might have flipped out. Do you know what happened to Sean? Why he was brain-damaged?"

"Some accident, I thought. When he was a baby."

"An accident caused by Jason McKendrick."

He whistled.

"You know what we think that means?"

He nodded. "First her mother, now her."

"Her mother?"

"Well, Sean's death flipped her out. The whole fam-ily's kind of . . . oh, well, I guess they had reason. What do you want Adrienne for?"

Chris said, "Whoever killed McKendrick did it with my car."

"Oh. Well."

"And then, a couple of nights ago, we were with some friends, and someone shot at us. It happened the day Adrienne ran away from the hospital."

"Boy, she's really flipped." It was a telling reaction, I thought. He might as easily have said, "Adrienne wouldn't do a thing like that."

"Can you think of anywhere she might have gone?

Is there anyone she felt she could trust? Who'd take care of her?''

He scratched his nose. ''Well, now that you mention it, yeah. Yeah, I think there might be somebody. But it might have been just one of Adrienne's stories. She always brought up this ex-boyfriend when she was mad at me. She said the guy would take her back in a minute; she liked to point out how rich he was. And famous—he's real famous, too. For a gangster.''

''What's his name?''

''Tommy La Barre.''

''Holy shit.'' I'd be a lousy poker player.

''Yeah. I never quite believed her on that one.'' He shrugged. ''But you never knew with Adrienne. Maybe it was true.''

Confronting a guy like Tommy La Barre wasn't my idea of a fun afternoon, but the fact that he'd seen me with Rob would help. At least he wouldn't kill someone so close to a reporter.

Where the hell *was* Rob, anyhow? I phoned him again; again no answer.

''I'm starving,'' said Chris. It was nearly two. ''Why don't we drop in to Dante's for a little something?''

''Sure. Maybe Adrienne's waiting tables over there.''

La Barre was sitting in exactly the same place Rob and I had found him before.

I hailed him. ''Tommy. Remember me?''

''Sure. The cub reporter. How's it going?''

''I got a weird tip. I heard you were involved with Jason McKendrick's assistant.''

His nasty little eyes glittered at me. ''You heard that, did you?''

''Yeah. I heard that.''

He didn't answer, just kept staring. For a while I held his gaze, but then I remembered that in my rational

moments I think staring contests are stupid. I smiled.
"Is it true?"

"No, it's not true."

I said, "Tommy, I think she killed Jason," and regretted it almost immediately. What if the two of them
were in it together? I'd been so caught up in the idea
of Adrienne as flipped-out freak I hadn't even thought
of it.

But something changed in his face, flickered in his
hard eyes. He said, "I loved that guy, you know?" and
I almost believed him. "Look, okay, she brought him
in here—that time he came to lunch—but I only saw her
once. I guess in a way she introduced me to Jason, so
I owe her. But if you mean this . . ."

"She brought him in here? Why would she bring him
if you didn't even know her?

"Because she knew all about me, and I knew all
about her. She wanted to meet me, she had some thing
about me, she even told people we were involved." He
shook his head. "Shit. Christ. I wouldn't be involved
with somebody that young. Uh-uh. Not this boy.
Women are like wine, you know what I mean? I like a
gal with some vintage on her." He leered, as he had
the first time we met. It was probably a habit.

"I feel like we're getting off the subject. How did
you two know all about each other?"

"Because my brother was fuckin' her."

"Your brother!"

"Shit, I don't care what happens to her. I don't even
care what happens to him." He stared at his glass and
brooded. "Dumb schmuck. Jason was my buddy."

"Are your brother and Adrienne in touch?"

"You mean now? Fuck no, she left him for some
faggoty kid."

"The kid says your brother wanted her back, he told

her he'd always take care of her. Only the kid thought
he was talking about you.''

Unexpectedly, Tommy La Barre leaned back and gave
a hard, bitter laugh. I had no idea what was so funny.
''Why don't you look him up? Why don't you girls just
go ask him? Fuck, I don't give a shit.'' He wrote a
name and address on one of his business cards.

As we turned toward the door, Chris said, ''No
lunch?''

''I can't eat on drugs.''

''The coffee? Mine's worn off.''

''Adrenaline. I think we're getting close.''

She sighed. ''I wish I did.''

I looked at the address. It was in the avenues, a funny
place, I thought, for a gangster's brother to live. It was
one of those stucco built-over-a-garage places that line
the streets out there, that stretch in unrelieved columns
for miles, that make you want to lose your lunch with
the sameness, the grim plainness of it all.

Yet they're perfectly nice houses, suitable for raising
sprawling urban families, and it came to me, as I looked
at the card with Tommy's brother's name on it—Edward
La Barre—that Edward might not be a bachelor.

Unfortunately, the thought was a little late, having
come a second or two after ringing the doorbell. The
woman who answered wore jeans and a tunic-length
T-shirt that looked as if it had been selected to hide a
belly curve that had arrived with a baby. Her hair was
black and curly, but slightly unkempt, as if she didn't
have time for grooming. It looked good that way, but I
was sure she couldn't be convinced of it, was probably
embarrassed at having been caught in weekend mode.
She was a handsome woman, substantial in weight, with
a deep, maternal bosom, against which she held what
was probably the latest of many babies.

"We're looking for Edward La Barre," I said.

"Tommy called." Anger flared from her eyes. "How dare you invade my house? How can you be so low?"

We started to back away.

"Coming to a person's house like this, after some punked-out little slut—how can you do a thing like that?"

How could Tommy La Barre set us up like this? That was the question. "I guess we made a mistake."

"Get out of here! Get out of here right now, goddamn it! Just leave. Just get out of here." The baby set up a howl I felt like joining.

"Okay, we're going. It's okay." We were more or less backing down the steps, but we didn't dare turn our backs.

Finally she slammed the door, and we turned toward each other to gibber in amazement at the thing that had befallen us. We had parked across the street, and I am quite sure no cars were in sight as we stepped off the curb, but we were caught slightly off guard, as we were much more interested in each other than the street. A light-colored car, no more than a blur of heavy machinery, bore down suddenly, motor purring, wind fairly whistling around it. We jumped backward, and the car was past. It kept speeding, remained a blur, and by this time we were interested in examining our skin, making sure it was intact; getting the license number was the last thing either of us thought of.

Yet when the shock had started to wear off—about thirty seconds down the line—we started to realize what had happened.

"Is it me," said Chris, "or did someone just try to run us down?"

"I think they must have pulled out of a parking place—that's why we didn't see them before."

"Does this have a familiar ring?"

It could have been Jason McKendrick all over again; *we* could have. But before I could speak, Mrs. La Barre came tearing out of the house. "Are you all right? Did she get you?"

"You saw the driver?"

"Who would it be but the slut? Look. Go talk to Eddie. What do I care? He doesn't see her anyway. He has way too much sense for the little bitch. He took the kids to the park. Go. Go see him."

"Thanks." I wasn't much in the mood, but I managed a kind of smile. "What park?"

"Golden Gate. Kristin likes the garden." She turned back.

"Could you tell us what your husband looks like?"

"No. No, I couldn't."

But a moment later she must have regretted her rudeness. "Just be careful," she called. "The slut's a killer."

"How do you know that?"

"Tommy told me you told him."

I sighed. That was how gossip got started.

CHAPTER 20

So off we went to a park nine blocks wide and four and a half miles long to find a man whose description we didn't have who was accompanied by an unknown number of children.

If they'd gone to Kristin's garden, that might narrow it down—probably they were somewhere near the Music Concourse. There were gardens all around there, some simple flower beds and others more formal. There was the Rhododendron Dell, but it wouldn't be in bloom now, so they probably weren't there. The Conservatory was fabulous, but we thought if that was what Kristin liked, Mrs. La Barre would have mentioned its name.

That left Strybing Arboretum and the Japanese Tea Garden. We opted for the latter because it had ''garden'' in its name and because it was by far the more exotic of the two, the more likely, we thought, to appeal to a kid. We had decided on the simple method of calling ''Eddie! Eddie La Barre!'' as if looking for a lost child, meanwhile keeping eyes peeled for a man with at least two children.

But if they were in the Japanese Tea Garden, they eluded us. We climbed the moon bridge and elbowed our way through the teahouse, making ourselves obnoxious to one and all, but to no avail.

Next, we tried Strybing Arboretum, which is quite a

bit bigger and harder to cover. We still had no luck. Undaunted, we popped over to the Garden of Shakespeare's Flowers, and then we did go to the Conservatory, knowing perfectly well that just because Kristin liked some garden or other didn't mean an entire family could spend a whole afternoon there. They could have gotten a quick hit of flowers and then gone rowing on Stow Lake for all we knew. It was starting to seem like a wild goose chase, but we couldn't see turning back at this point—though Chris did insist on getting a hot dog before trekking to the Conservatory.

We entered the giant wedding cake, calling lightly, "Eddie? Eddie, where are you? Eddie La Barre! Oh, Eddieeeee." It must have driven the other park goers nuts.

But it worked.

A man's voice said, "Who's that? I'm in here—who's calling me?"

We followed it into the Pond Room, which was like a rain forest dripping tropical moisture, hot and sensuous. We could barely see anyone through the steamy mist. "Who's that?" said the voice.

And we saw a man, a short, thick blond man who looked enough like Tommy La Barre to be his twin. He had four children with him, three of them clinging, apparently unnerved by the strange voices calling their dad. There were three boys and one little girl, a gorgeous thin little creature with hair that was neither thick and blond like her dad's nor thick and black like her mother's, but brown and wavy. She was dressed, not in a T-shirt and jeans, but in a sort of organza skirt topped with what looked like a bathing suit top. She was clearly at the age of dress-up, four or five, I thought.

The boys were small, though one may have been as old as ten, and they were dark like their mother, with finely wrought features. Genes, I thought, are wonderful things, and reflected that I'd really never seen an ugly child.

Eddie La Barre was a father of five and had recently had an affair with a twenty-three-year-old. It was a good escape, I guessed, but the memory of his angry, harried wife made it seem ugly and cheap, terribly unfair.

The little girl smiled. "We're playing rain forest," she said. "Watch out for the alligators, Ooooh, watch out!"

"You must be Kristin."

"Uh-huh. You want to get in our boat? We're going down the Amazon."

The oldest boy blushed, caught playing with babies.

The man said, "I'm Eddie La Barre. You were calling me?"

"Your wife told us where you were."

Alarm showed on his face, something, despite the brothers' similarities, that probably wasn't in Tommy's repertoire. "Is something wrong?"

"Not at all. We got your name from your brother. We wanted to talk to you, that's all."

And then a refinery exploded about ten feet away.

Or so it seemed.

La Barre pushed the kids to the ground and dropped, all four children screaming at once. We heard shouts and scurrying throughout the glass house, but Chris and I stood riveted, heads swiveling, unable to grasp what had happened.

Finally La Barre, catching on that we were sitting ducks, shouted, "Get down! Someone's shooting." There was another explosion. I dropped and heard Chris do the same; my only thought, wildly, crazily, not for us or the children, but for the marvelous old building: Oh, God, not in here!

"Daddy!" shouted someone. "Daddy, stop!"

It was not a child's voice, but a young woman's I couldn't place. Chris whispered: "Adrienne," and I raised my head, but I couldn't see anyone through the mist.

"Daddy, give me the gun. It's okay, you don't have to shoot anybody."

"Adrienne, you stay out of this. I don't want to hurt you."

"You came to get me, didn't you? Well, here I am. I'm right here, and everything's fine. We'll go home now. We'll go home and have a nice drink. Come on, Dad—it's too hot to be out here. Maybe a Long Island iced tea."

"I got the reporter; now I got to get the lawyers. *Then* everything'll be fine. It's not fine yet, Adrienne. You go home now."

Eddie La Barre called, "Adrienne, go!"

"Who's that?" Dunson's voice changed, became the voice of a crazy man, paranoid, on edge.

"Dad, come on, now. Give me the gun and let's go."

Ignoring her, he stepped into view. I could see him from the back, staring at Eddie, down on the ground with his children. "Whoever you are, you've got four kids. Hey, Adrienne, who is this guy?"

Adrienne walked into view also, but I noticed she didn't get too close to her dad. "Dad, it doesn't matter—let's just go now." She held out a hand but kept her distance.

"Stand up, mister."

La Barre stood, but I heard him whispering to his kids: "Stay down. Don't move."

"You've got three beautiful boys, and I don't have any. Hey, Adrienne, I can solve this thing. I'll just take one of his boys."

"Dad, I don't think that's a good idea." Adrienne

spoke, not as if her father had suddenly snapped, but like a woman used to dealing with crazy people. I wondered what her life had been like and didn't envy her.

She stepped closer to the children.

Her father said, "You kids. Stand up."

"No." Adrienne and Eddie La Barre spoke at once.

"Come on, Daddy." Again she held out her hand.

"Adrienne, you're in my way."

"We've really got to go home now."

"Adrienne, don't make me shoot you." He fired again, another of those hideous blasts I feared would shatter the building.

She jumped at him, grabbed for his gun, and once again it went off. Adrienne's body twitched and sank to the floor.

Dunson yelled, apparently to the world at large, "Now look what you made me do! I had a son, a wife, and a daughter, and now I don't have anybody. I'm taking a kid. You owe me that."

He kicked one of the children. "You. Get up."

The little boy didn't move.

He kicked another. "You!"

The kid made an "oof" noise.

"Come on, or I'll kick you again."

I followed the kid's eyes to the still body of Adrienne, blood oozing from her upper chest. Seizing the opportunity, Dunson shouted. "Get up or I'll shoot you."

The kid stood and Dunson had him in an instant, his left arm pinning the kid against his body.

Without thinking, I stood up. "Mr. Dunson."

He whirled, and I saw the madness in his eyes.

"I thought you wanted me. That's what you told Adrienne. I heard you."

"The lawyer."

"Look, take me instead of the kid."

"But they got my son."

"They got your wife, too."

His face lit up. I hadn't thought such a thing could happen in the circumstances. "I could kill two birds with one stone."

I smiled. At least I worked my face in smilelike fashion; I can't vouch for the effect. "Let the boy go, okay?"

"You come over here."

My legs shook, but I did. He shoved the boy aside and grabbed me in one motion. "Let's get out of here."

And then we were running, running past horrified onlookers, our fellow Conservatory visitors, then just running, toward his car, I supposed. Sirens were starting somewhere in the distance.

A little too late, I thought. Just a little too late.

Since then I've wondered often if I should have struggled at that point, tried to break away, but my only thought was to get him out of the park. He had shot his own daughter and might shoot anyone, I thought, anyone or everyone, child or adult. I just wanted him out of there.

And yet we had to go somewhere. It didn't occur to me that no matter where he took me, people would still be in danger.

He found a baseball cap in his car and jerked it on. It changed his appearance just enough, perhaps. He made me drive so that he could keep the gun trained on me, giving directions at every corner.

I was less afraid for the moment, and my heart slowed a little, knowing he probably wouldn't shoot me now, not while his own life depended on my being alive.

I had time now to think, and I couldn't get something he'd said off my mind: "I got the reporter."

How was I supposed to interpret that? I shivered and tried to get it out of my mind. I needed to focus.

The man sitting next to me was so crazy he'd shot his only daughter, but perhaps there was some ounce of sanity left in him, some tiny speck of conscience that I could appeal to. I said, "Adrienne's dead, I think."

"Bullshit. I wouldn't kill Adrienne."

"But there's a very good chance you did. You shot her in the chest."

"Shut up!"

He broke the silence every now and then to give me directions. Once we were safely on the Bay Bridge, heading back to the East Bay, I tried again. "How did your wife die?"

"Suicide, goddammit. You know that."

"After Sean died?"

He shook his head, but not, I realized, to signify a negative. It was the shake of sadness that people give. "It damn near killed her." And then, realizing what he had said, he gave a mirthless hoot. "It did kill her. We had an old gun I kept around just in case. One day she ate it for lunch, right in front of me." His head went from side to side—shake, shake, shake—as if the horror of it had loosened his neck bones.

"McKendrick killed Sean, and he killed Carlene. Bastard!"

"He deserved to die, I guess."

"Damn right he did!"

"You must have gotten the keys to my partner's car when you went to visit Adrienne at her office."

"Of course I did. It was the perfect setup."

"But my partner was innocent. She could have gone to prison for a murder you committed."

"First of all, you just said it yourself—it wasn't fuckin' murder. It was an execution. He killed my son,

I killed him; that simple. And so what about your damned partner? I lost Sean, and then I lost Carlene. Why shouldn't the inside lose two of theirs?''

''The inside?''

''Yeah, the inside. You know what it's like to have a vegetable for a son? To spend every fuckin' nickel you make trying to keep him alive when he's never going to talk or think or do anything except shit his pants? Carlene insisted on that. That's why it hit her so hard when he died. She got born again after the accident, and she just knew Jesus wasn't going to let her down. He was going to come right down from heaven and make her baby well again. Instead, he sent a lifetime of seizures and a case of pneumonia.''

I was losing the thread. ''But what's the inside?''

''Everything but us, missy. That's the inside. Having Sean like that, having to live like that made us outsiders. Look at Adrienne! The girl dresses in black all the time. She's not normal. There's nothing normal about that girl. How could there be? Her little brother's skull got cracked when she was five years old. How the fuck was she supposed to be normal?''

''Adrienne's dead, Mr. Dunson. You got one on the outside too.''

''Adrienne is not dead! I wouldn't kill my own daughter.''

Would you kill my friend Rob?

I didn't have the courage to ask.

As we got off the bridge, I said, ''Where to now?''

''Just listen, that's all. I'll tell you a little bit at a time.''

When I found myself looking out at the City from the East Bay hills, taking in the view of three bridges from Tilden Park, I realized where he was taking me.

CHAPTER 21

"We're going to Inspiration Point, aren't we?"

"How did you know that?"

"Because I met Jason's brother, Michael. He told me all about the accident and how it tore his family apart; how they never recovered from it. They became outsiders, too, you know. The parents died young—and so did Jason, of course. The sister's a dry husk of a woman, and Michael's either an alcoholic or headed toward it."

"I'm supposed to care? Look at me? I've been an alcoholic for fifteen years! You know what my wife had to put up with? Goddammit, she was a saint."

"Why are we going to Inspiration Point?"

"I'm going to kill you there."

No clever rejoinder came to mind.

"You are Carlene today. She died, and you are going to die."

"And you?" I had an idea this was it for him as well.

He nodded. "And I am, too."

I couldn't help thinking of the Indian summer day nearly two decades ago, not much later in the season than this, when the impulse of a moment, a young boy's desire to see his dog run free, had started a chain of events that destroyed the lives of two families. At least two of the Dunsons were dead as a result—possibly three—and so was one McKendrick. Maybe Rob was too and perhaps I would be in a few minutes. It was so senseless, all this; it reminded me of the feud in *Huckleberry Finn*.

"What's your name?" said Dunson. "I've forgotten."

"Rebecca."

"Today, Rebecca, you represent Carlene Dunson, who lived in horror and died in horror. It's all I can do for her now."

That enraged me so much I couldn't keep my mouth shut. "You're going to kill me for her? You really think she'd want that? The saint? You think she'd have wanted you to kill your own daughter?"

"I didn't kill Adrienne." We were stopped now, in the parking lot of the Point. "Give me the keys."

He took them and stared at his gun a moment. "Stay in the car until I get to your side."

I hated myself for obeying, for remaining passive, but I couldn't see an alternative. There was no way to slide under the wheel, out one bucket seat and into another, then out the opposite door before he got there. There was nothing to do but sit and drum my fingers, contemplate my own mortality. It made me furious, having to submit that way.

When I did get out, he took my hand and slipped the gun in his pocket.

"What are you doing?"

"I'm taking you for a walk. We're going to hold hands because I can't keep the gun on you right now."

He guided me to the path that Jason and his siblings had taken the day of the accident, the path Dunson had taken as well on his bicycle, his baby son strapped on behind.

We walked. It was a beautiful day just like that other one, and plenty of hikers were out. There were people

on bicycles as well, and some dogs, safely on leashes.
Such a peaceful scene, yet so much capacity for havoc.
I felt a physical ache, almost, at seeing the elements
laid out like this, so ironically, so vividly. Thinking
about it, that fateful moment eighteen years go, I felt
tears well and I had to sniff. Dunson yanked my arm;
why, I wasn't sure. I sneaked a glance at him, and his
face was hard.

We walked. The sun was pure luxury on our skin. I
had no idea how far he intended to walk, and what he
would do—perhaps he would simply blow my head off
without announcing his plans. One second I'd be walking under a benign sun, the next I'd be dead. I could
worry about that or I could enjoy the walk. In retrospect, it seems preposterous that I didn't worry with
every atom of every cell, but we walked a long time
Perhaps endorphins kicked in. I really can't explain it,
all I can say is that I experienced a very ill-advised
sense of well-being, that even under the circumstances
I couldn't close myself off to the pleasures of the day.

My hand stopped feeling sweaty in his, started actually to feel companionable. This was, after all, another human being, and my skin was touching his.
Perhaps it was the beginning of the Stockholm Syndrome, I don't know. I just know that for the first time
I was aware of Dunson as a man rather than a monster.

"You can't kill a person you've held hands with," I
blurted.

"Shut up."

"You're not a killer, I know that."

"Crazy bitch," he yelled, but not at me. Looking
where his eyes were trained, I saw that a young girl had
just loosed her dog, a terrier that looked as if it had ten
or twelve hell-bent-for-leather miles in it before it would
even start to flag. In half a second the dog was a blur.

The girl stood transfixed, staring at Dunson.

"You crazy, crazy, *crazy* bitch. You can't let that dog run loose. Don't you know what can happen on a trail like this?"

The girl couldn't have been more than sixteen. Her skin looked as if she'd grown up on the Shetland Islands, perhaps, someplace with heavy fog. Her hair was blond and short. She was slender, almost wispy. I half expected her to flee in alarm, but she only shrugged. "So arrest me."

For a moment I thought he would, knew he considered it. I almost encouraged him but remembered in time that he was crazy. The distraction might save my life, but it could endanger hers. He would probably train the gun on her, and might very well shoot. Go! I wanted to shout. Go catch your dog—anything. But get out of here fast.

I didn't, though, didn't dare cause a scene.

The dog came galloping back, it's energy not even slightly spent, a force of nature set free, more gale-force wind than animal. There were bicycles on the path, as there had been that other time, but the dog made it safely back to its owner, stopped to be petted, and took off again.

I had an idea. It was a crazy idea, and dangerous, but I was damned if I was going to walk quietly to my own execution. I looked around for what I needed, and saw it, a few steps ahead. If only the dog would return . . .

"Bijou! Here, Bijou." The girl was calling her pet, who surely must have been a puppy. It turned around more or less in mid-gallop, and came tearing back toward us. Dunson was nearly apoplectic, too intent on the dog to pay much attention to me.

"Get that goddamn dog on a leash, or I swear I'll make a citizen's arrest!"

I swooped down and picked up the stick I'd spotted. "Bijou!" Hearing its name, the dog inclined its head toward me. I threw the stick, and luck was with me—a bicycle was heading down the path, on a collision course with Bijou.

Dunson apparently forgot me completely, forgot the whole purpose of the mission, went crazy in an entirely different way. He let go of my hand and took off after the dog, the girl and me chasing him. I tried to stop her. "Call the police! He's got a gun. Get out of here—please!" She kept coming. But other hikers started to scatter, and the oncoming cyclist began to wobble on her bike. Bijou, completely oblivious, kept galloping, and at that moment, another cyclist came into view, coasting down a small incline, wind in his face, having a fabulous time and suffering absolutely no notion of the pandemonium in his path. The stick landed right in front of him.

Bijou and Dunson arrived at nearly the same time, with me a millisecond behind. Though I'd never played football in my life, I launched my body at Dunson in what I imagined was a flying tackle; I caught him around the pelvis and we leaned forward . . . leaned, leaned, and finally fell. Bijou jumped out of the way, escaping so narrowly that I saw her brown paw come down inches from my face. The cyclist flying down the hill ran over us.

Or at least he would have if he'd been on a motorcycle, but the bicycle overturned as soon as it hit Dunson's shoulder, and fell on top of us, the rider barely managing not to. Still, it hurt. It hurt me, and I didn't get the brunt of it. It hurt Dunson more, I hoped, and better yet it pinned him. I groped in his pockets, reaching for the gun.

"Stop that, goddamn it! This woman's trying to rob me!" But the bicycle held his right arm, and his own body had pinned his left.

I pulled the gun out and jammed it into his lower back as hard as I could, exactly as I'd seen in the movies: "Freeze or I'll blow your ass off."

Considering that he was planning to kill himself, it wasn't much of a threat, but he froze just long enough for me to pick myself up and get to my knees. "Okay, stand back everybody. Somebody call the police." The cyclist got out of the way. I rose carefully, the gun trained at the middle of Dunson's back.

He still couldn't move without a great upheaval of metal and wheels, but he twisted his face around. "Is Adrienne okay?" he said. "Where's Adrienne?"

"You killed her, you fucker." Good-bye Stockholm Syndrome; I wasn't cutting him one inch of slack. "What did you do with Rob Burns?"

"Rob Burns? Who's Rob Burns?"

"The reporter."

"Oh, him. He's at my house."

I swallowed. "What did you do with him?"

"What do you mean what did I do with him?"

"He's dead, isn't he? You killed him." I shouldn't have asked. I felt dizzy, watched his face go out of focus.

"No, I didn't kill him. Why would I kill him? I just tied him up to get him out of the way."

"You didn't kill him?" I was aware I was gibbering, also smiling, poor strategy while holding someone at gunpoint.

"Hey, watch it. Watch it! Let me take that, okay?" The spilled cyclist was trying to get macho. I couldn't really blame him—my gun was shaking a little—but no late-arriving Ken Doll was getting it away from me.

"You want to try to take it?" I said. "Go ahead, make my day." Since I avoid clichés whenever possible, I forebore to add "punk."

And so we waited for the cops, Dunson and me, a frozen tableau, as fascinating, judging from the thickening crowds, as the Mona Lisa.

After about a millennium, the police came.

A century or so after that, I persuaded them to go get Rob, and three years later, Chris joined us at the police station. A month after that they released us.

Acting on some good news Chris had brought, we headed for San Francisco General.

Adrienne had a hole in her shoulder, but she was out of surgery and conscious by the time the three of us could get to her.

She was dead-white, still pretty doped up, but she managed to smile. "You're all alive."

"You're the one we were worried about."

Her face darkened. "Is Dad okay?"

"He's been arrested, but he's fine."

"He shot me. My own dad shot me."

"He didn't mean to, Adrienne. Your dad's pretty out of it."

"For Christ's sake, Rebecca," said Chris. "Stop making excuses for him. He's her dad, and he tried to kill her—she's got to live with that."

Adrienne nodded. "Thank you." Some of the trouble left her face. I realized that it wasn't the time to take the side of the man who'd done this to her—and that it must have sounded as if I had.

"I tried to cover for him," she said.

"We know. You must have figured out he'd killed Jason when you noticed the keys missing."

"Uh-huh." She couldn't seem to say anymore.

"You're tired, aren't you? Do you want us to leave?"

"No!" Her voice was much stronger. "Please don't leave me."

I felt for her. She was twenty-three, and she'd lost so many people, so much. She'd lost nearly everything. I hoped it wasn't too late for her, that her life could start again.

She said, "I found out . . . I don't want to die."

"You took the pills rather than turn your dad in?"

She nodded, looking grateful we understood. "And then, when he came to the hospital, I tried to get him to give himself up. And he went nuts. He didn't know I knew, you see. So he . . ." She searched for the right word. "He took me."

"He kidnapped you."

"I guess so. I guess that's what it was. He locked me in a room." Her eyes filled, and she fought for control for a minute; then she turned to Rob. "What were you doing there?"

"I was watching the house. Waiting for you to show up. Then I saw you two doors down. . . ."

"I got loose and went out the back door. I just stayed in backyards till I thought it was safe."

"Brilliant me." Rob was speaking to Chris and me. "I hailed her, which alerted the old man." He smiled ruefully. "Adrienne got away, but I didn't."

"I had to get some gas, though, and that slowed me down.

"Dad went through my things when he took me from the hospital. So he knew about Eddie from a journal I had. I found out where Eddie was from Tommy, who'd already talked to you and Chris, Rebecca. I guess Dad followed me to the park, and we all ended up in the Conservatory at the same time.''

"He must have talked to Eddie's wife. That's how we got there.''

Adrienne said, "Poor woman. I wish . . .''

Her strength seemed to fail then. She couldn't complete the sentence, but I knew what she wished.

She wished she could have found someone to love her who wasn't already taken.

She wished she hadn't been so desperate that her only friend in the world was somebody else's husband.

She wished her mom was alive, and her brother.

She wished her dad hadn't tried to kill her.

She wished Jason McKendrick hadn't let his stupid dog off its miserable leash on a gorgeous sunny day eighteen years before.

The novels of **JULIE SMITH**
are available in your local bookstore.

Published by Ivy Books.

NEW ORLEANS MOURNING

It's Mardi Gras in New Orleans, and hysterical revelers crowd the street to see the prominent Chauncey St. Amant, who has been crowned the King of the Carnical. Then a costumed killer murders Chauncey, and policewoman Skip Langdon is on the case. Skip is the daughter of social-climbing parents, and she knows only too well the byzantine politics of New Orleans society. But nothing could prepare Skip for the web of tangled clues and ancient secrets at the heart of this mystery.

THE AXEMAN'S JAZZ

Among the ranks of the hundreds of self-help groups in New Orleans, a deadly serial killer is at large. So off goes the intrepid Skip Langdon threading her fascinated way from one self-help group to another in search of a dangerously attractive psychopath.

JAZZ FUNERAL

The beloved producer of the New Orleans Jazz and Heritage Festival has been murdered, and homicide detective Skip Langdon is on the trail of a cold-blooded killer. Is the missing sister a victim, or is she the killer? With the help of her long-distance love and her eccentric landlord, Skip is determined to break this case before it breaks her.

JULIE SMITH

DEAD IN THE WATER
Attorney Rebecca Schwartz is admiring the kelp tank at a world famous aquarium when a dead body floats into view. Rebecca's friend, Marty, is the prime suspect so Rebecca takes the case and discovers there is a psycho loose with more than mackerel on the mind.

DEATH TURNS A TRICK
It's one thing to represent hookers in court and quite another to play piano for fun at a feminist co-op bordello. San Francisco attorney Rebecca Schwartz nearly gets arrested in a phony police raid and comes home to find a slain prostitute in her apartment. And then she discovers a killer is on her trail.

THE SOURDOUGH WARS
Peter Martinelli, owner of a renowned sourdough recipe, is murdered before he can auction the recipe off. Rebecca Schwartz wants to know if he really died for a handful of dough, but she must use all of her resources to keep herself alive to find out.

TOURIST TRAP
A man identifying himself as "the Trapper" is out to destroy San Francisco's tourist business by killing visitors. Attorney Rebecca Schwartz is determined to save her beloved adopted city and prevent an innocent man from going to jail.

JULIE SMITH